Secret Bells

Marsha Sabin Pester

Cover & interior design by Typewriter Creative Co.

Front cover image generated from Canva AI
Back cover image from Cottonbro Studio on Pexels.com

ISBN 979-8-9871053-6-8 (Paperback)
ISBN 979-8-9871053-7-5 (eBook)

*This book is lovingly dedicated
to the memory
of my best friend
and husband,
John.*

Prologue

1651

"Eliza! Hurry with that sewing. The men are ready to leave. I don't intend to be left behind."

"Yes, My Lady. I'm about finished." Eliza, maid to Lady Rosalind, was just sewing the last of eight secret pockets in an underskirt. Each pocket contained a small silver bell. She had first wrapped strips of cloth around the clapper of each bell to prevent it from sounding. For the past several days Eliza had secreted rings, bracelets, and other valuables into various pieces of clothing.

Civil war raged across England. In 1649, King Charles I had been beheaded by the Puritans, who now ruled Parliament under Oliver Cromwell. Lady Rosalind stopped what she was doing, balled her hands into fists and wailed at no one in particular, "Those ignorant Roundheads with their silly looking short hair!"

Eliza kept her head down and continued sewing. She wasn't sure who the Roundheads were but knew that since they had come into power, many things had changed. The family no longer held elegant dinner parties or dances. There were no nights out to the theater. Even the church services had changed. Elizabeth, Eliza's cousin, had come to visit her Monday last. She had asked, "Isn't Lady Rosalind related to old King Charles? I heard in town that the Puritan army is killing all the Royalists." Eliza had been sworn to secrecy by Lady Rosalind not to tell anyone the family was preparing to leave England. Because the master was a distant cousin of the slain king, he had decided to seek refuge in the new world.

"I'm finished, My Lady."

"Don't just sit there like a simpleton. Can't you hear the uproar outside? Put the dress and undergarment on. There isn't time to pack them. Grab my case."

Eliza's jaw dropped. She sat stunned not believing what Lady Rosalind had just told her. Lady Rosalind seized Eliza by her shoulders almost knocking her over, "Do as I say, you ninny."

Eliza could hear yelling and screaming coming from the front portico. Above the racket she thought she heard her master yelling for them to hide. She finally came to her senses and put on the dress. Lady Rosalind was frantically looking around the room for a place to hide.

No sooner had Eliza downed the lovely garment when she heard wood splintering and glass breaking. There was the sound of heavy boots, more screams and crying and men angrily shouting.

The boudoir door was opened so violently it hit the wall. The master stood in the doorway. He grabbed the doorpost with his left, blood-covered hand. He held his right hand tightly across his chest. A great amount of blood was streaming between his fingers. He looked wildly at Rosalind. Opening his mouth to speak, only blood streamed out. His knees buckled and he fell into Rosalind's arms. They dropped to the floor. Rosalind tenderly embraced him, bowed her head over the now dead man and sobbed.

A soldier stumbled over the couple as he entered the room. He regained his balance and surveyed the scene. He stood opened mouthed and dumbfounded. It was more luxurious than he thought could exist in the whole world. Intricate tapestries hung from the walls. Strewn across amazingly crafted furniture were gowns of dazzling colors and designs. Anger surged through him as he thought of the squalor his family endured. It wasn't right that some creatures should live such privileged lives while his babies went to bed each night crying from hunger. With pursed lips he raised his knife and thrust it into Lady Rosalind's back. Mortally wounded she collapsed onto her husband. Disregarding Eliza, the soldier gave a wicked laugh as he pulled the knife from Rosalind. He jumped over the pair and continued his journey of mayhem.

Eliza stood petrified with fear. Lady Rosalind looked up at her. In her dying moment she uttered, "Run, Eliza, run. Save yourself." Eliza fled still holding Lady Rosalind's case.

She raced out the wide French doors onto a marbled veranda surrounded by potted flowering plants. Leaping over the masonry stonework, she knocked over two pots in her haste. Fleeing down a gravel pathway and through the shrub and terraced grounds, she reached a forest. Flying until her legs gave out, she dropped to the cold ground, not daring to move. Sun-light filtered through ancient oak, ash, and beech trees while she lay surrounded by the scent of moss and decaying leaves. In the distance Eliza heard fighting and death.

Then, there was total silence.

Eliza rose to her feet. She had grown up in this forest. It was her friend and did not frighten her with its sounds and animal inhabitants. She knew exactly where she was. She started to slowly walk then realized she had lost a shoe. She couldn't even remember when that had happened.

The ship the family had hired to take them to safety was moored on the river, a short journey to the north. It wouldn't do much good to go there. She surely wouldn't be allowed on board without her mistress. But she did know of other smaller ship owners.

Perhaps one of them would help her. They would require money. That was when she realized she still carried Lady Rosalind's case. What had her lady put in it? Could Eliza trade some of the contents for a ride to safety?

Eliza unlashed the lid and drew out a night gown, several lace-trimmed handkerchiefs, and papers with fancy words. Since Eliza had never learned to read, the papers held no interest to her. Something softly clinked as she set the papers aside.

Coins! Eliza had rarely seen a farthing. Here were nestled coins of all kinds, copper, silver and even some gold ones. She had no inkling of their value but it must be a lot. She let them run through her fingers like water.

Another thought struck her. She would be murdered for the coins if anyone learned she had them. If only she had brought her sewing basket with her! Instead, after she could think of no better ideas, one by one, she carefully stuffed the coins between her shift and corset.

She spent the night in the hollow of a tree getting very little sleep. The horror of what she had witnessed that day played over and over in her mind. She felt guilty. Was there something she could or should have done to help her mistress? Was she a coward for running? Hadn't her mistress told her to? Was she wrong in keeping the coins? She rationalized. The coins were of no use to her mistress. The coins, they were so uncomfortable.

Eliza was awakened after a fitful night. Hunger gnawed at her. She crawled out of the hollow stiff and cold. The hidden coins poked in to her like minute bits of torture.

What had happened, was it only yesterday, rushed back to her. She wanted to cry but what good would that do? Groaning she picked up her mistress's case, discarded her one shoe and walked to the town of her birth.

Eliza had no family left. Both parents were dead and her only sister had married and lived in the country. She made her way to a second-hand shop. As she entered the shop, a woman with an extremely bent back shuffled from behind a curtained door. The proprietrix recognized Eliza. "Well, lookie who we have here. I thought all you high-and-mighties got your come-upends yesterday."

Eliza ignored the comment, "Mrs. Smythe, I need your help. May I have something to drink, please? And if you could spare a crust of bread, I would so appreciate your kindness."

Mrs. Smythe looked Eliza over. Although disheveled, the dress she wore could not be hers. She saw the shoeless feet, then she spied the lavish travel case. As sincerely as Mrs. Smythe's hard personality would allow, she beamed, "My Dear, come in. You look like you have experienced something awful. Come into my back room and tell Auntie Jane all about it."

Eliza was emotionally drained. She poured out her sad story to Mrs. Smythe while consuming slices of black bread, commonly called Carter's bread, a large chunk of cheese and some weak ale. She was not so distressed or witless as to reveal her secret about the hidden coins.

Mrs. Smythe was generally known as an honest dealer in second-hand merchandise. Then again, she knew an opportunity when it presented itself. She asked to see the contents of the case. "Oh, my dear, your mistress must have feared taking her best things. These are not of high quality. I'll show you what I'll trade for them."

Eliza knew Mrs. Smythe wasn't being honest. "Mrs. Smythe, I appreciate your kindness to me. However, I know that all my lady's things were of good quality. All I ask is shoes, and a hat. And I need to sponge off this dress and fix my hair."

After dickering with Mrs. Smythe for with seemed to Eliza an eternity, she was able to trade the case, night gown, and hankies for a rather remarkable hat and a pair of shoes. The cavalier style chapeau was blue and broad-brimmed. It was flamboyant with feathers in various colors. Her shoes were dyed pink leather and embellished with embroidery. The heels were two inches high with pink ribbon ties across the instep. Lace and ribbon rosettes were sewn onto the top front of each shoe. When Eliza slipped them on, she danced around at how well they fit.

Now she resembled a respectable upper-class lady, how-be-it, a little out of present style. A plan began to form in her mind. She would need help from a man. She knew just the man to ask.

She strolled to a local butcher. The butcher's son had been sweet on Eliza. If he still worked for his father and hadn't married, maybe he would help her.

The shop's window remained mostly obscured by hanging fowl and several kinds of sausages just like when she had lived there. Eliza spotted the butcher and his son arguing. People gathered in front of the shop observing the commotion. Eventually, the son stormed out, pushed through the crowd, and charged down the street passing Eliza without recognizing her.

"Joseph! Joseph!"

Joseph turned and glared. "Eliza? Is that you? Where did you get that get-up?"

Eliza put her finger to her lips and carefully glanced around, "Joseph, is there someplace safe we can talk?"

Joseph scanned the area and beckoned with his head for her to follow him. He turned into a dark narrow alleyway. Buildings on either side hung haphazardly over the thoroughfare preventing sun from inserting itself into the path.

Half-way down, Joseph cracked opened a door and waited for Eliza to go in.

A musty scent assaulted her as she entered the tiny dim room. Only a scant bit of sunlight managed to enter a dirty windowpane.

With hands on his hips, Joseph turned to Eliza, "Now tell me what's going on."

She had to employ Joseph's voice to locate him as her eyes adjusted to the darkened room.

"We heard rumors that the Roundheads had attacked the manner house and took everyone prisoner."

Eliza's handed fisted at her collar as yesterday's scene unfolded in her mind.

"They did attack. We were readying to flee. Before we could though they came and killed the master and my Lady. With her dying breath, she told me to run. So, I did." Eliza swayed and grasped for Joseph. Her legs, like her hopes were about to give out.

"I've got you, girl. I've got you."

Oh, to hold on to him, but there was no time. "Joseph, I'm so afraid. I need your help!"

"What can I do?"

"The master and my lady were planning on leaving for the place they called Maryland. It's across the ocean in the new world. Can you read?"

"Some. Why?"

"I have papers that I found in my lady's case." She pulled a rolled bundle of papers from between her breasts. "Here. What do they say?"

Joseph's eyes couldn't help opening wide as he saw Eliza reveal a large portion of her beautiful breasts. He took the papers trying hard not to stare and unwillingly strode to where a little light that had managed to penetrate the room. He used his elbow to scrub the window-pane the best he could. Silently he mouthed the words as he slowly read the contents. His finger moved along the lettering helping him to follow the writing. Finally, after several minutes he said, "If I've read this right, these are letters from some man named Lord Baltimore giving permission for your master to come to Maryland. They were to sail on the *Dove*. It leaves from Margate in two days. There is passage here for the master, his ladyship and two servants."

"I was to be one of the servants!" Then before she could change her mind, she added, "Come with me, Joseph. You can be the other servant!"

Open mouthed, he glared at Eliza. "Now why should I do that? And who will be the master and his lady? And how do we get to Margate?"

"I know you don't like it here. I have money! We can hire a coach. We'll make up a story about the master coming later. Then when the ship is to leave, we'll just stay on somehow. Please, Joseph."

"I have a better idea. Do you have enough money to buy me some nice clothes, like you're wearing? I will be the master and you, my lady."

"Yes, Joseph, I do! Think we can do it?" Eliza wanted to jump up and down or even better, hug and kiss Joseph. She could hardly believe what Joseph was saying.

"I've watched the gentry swagger about all my life. Put me in the right kind of clothes, and no one will doubt me." Then he came over to Eliza, picked her up and swung her around. "We can do it! My lady!" As he put her down, they smiled at each other. Eliza started to giggle. Soon both were laughing.

Eliza and Joseph made it to Maryland. They were married three days after landing. With the money Eliza had, they bought land and built a butcher shop and a fine house. Eliza put the silver bells on the mantle. Their first child, Margate, was born in 1652.

Eliza gave Margate the bells when she married. Johanna, Margate's daughter received the bells on her wedding day in 1689. Each birthday she allowed her children to celebrate using the bells.

It became a tradition in the family for each mother to give the bells to her first daughter. Johanna bore Hephzibah in 1690. Hephzibah received the bells in 1713.

They were passed to Hephzibah's daughter, Victoria, in 1735. In 1760, Jane received them from her mother, Victoria. Jane gave them to her first daughter, Claribel, in 1776.

Claribel married a British soldier, Andrew Ogden. He had been born in the colonies and was loyal to the revolutionary cause. When the war for independence from England began, he discharged himself from the British army. He and Claribel headed west. Their first stop was the Ohio valley. Andrew and Claribel Ogden continued to move about. In thirty-seven years of marriage, they produced fourteen children.

The tradition of passing the bells from mother to oldest daughter continued down through the years. Sometime during this time one of the bells was lost.

Chapter 1

1928

"Miss Claire, wake-up. There are people downstairs asking for you." Claire groggily lifted her head, pushed back her tangled hair and glanced at the bedside clock. It was 2:45 a.m. Who in the world would be calling in the middle of the night? It must be bad news.

"Alright, Ann, I'm awake. Quit shaking me. Who's downstairs? Is someone crying?"

"Yes, Miss. It's a baby and her mother wants to see you. Mr. Pierce is talking to her now."

"My father is up?" Claire couldn't fathom what was going on. Several possibilities race through her mind, none of them credible. Ann helped her on with her robe. "Does he know the woman?"

"I think so Miss. He is very upset. He woke up with all the pounding the woman was making at the door. He called me and said to get you. Here are your slippers. Please hurry."

Claire sighed. She couldn't imagine who would be here at two in the morning. She and Ann, one of the Pierce family's two maids, hurried down the stairs to the foyer.

The two-storied foyer was large and grand. A round mahogany table sat in the center of the marble flooring. Gold metallic aviary prints with blooming flowers and birds on the wing covered the walls. The winding staircase terminated on the left, where an arched opening led to Anthony Pierce's office and bedroom suite.

Claire's great-grandparents had commissioned the building of the house in 1838. In 1900 Claire had been born in this house, twenty-eight years ago. So had her two sisters and brother. Her father and grandfather had also begun life here. Originally it had been the only house for several miles around. Now, in 1928, it was surrounded by several other large homes, though none as grand.

Claire stopped on the bottom stair and surveyed the scene. Her father, Anthony Pierce, stood with his back to Claire, talking to a woman with flaming fuzzy red hair. The red appeared to have come from a bottle. The woman had an angular face and a prominent jaw. Her figure was generous and pear-shaped. Nothing about her was attractive. Dark bags hung below her eyes that were wide with fear. She looked scared and tired. In her arms was a whimpering baby. A very dirty boy, who looked to be about eight or nine, stood off to one side. A girl, equally dirty, who appeared to be about two or three, clung to the woman's dress.

"Father?"

Mr. Pierce turned, "Oh, Claire, I'm glad you're up. This is Nadine Johnson Rainy Taft. Do you remember her? She's a distant cousin."

Before Claire could reply, Nadine moved past Mr. Pierce to Claire. The little girl, still holding onto her mother's dress, stumbled along with her. The boy continued to stand off to one side, ogling the foyer. "Claire! You remember me, don't you? I spent a summer here with you when we were just kids. You remember, don't you? Please, say you do."

"Yes." Claire hesitated before continuing as a fragment of memory returned, "I kind of do. It was when we were about ten. Why are you here now, in the middle of the night? Are these your children?"

"Yes! Yes! Claire, I need your help." Just then a horn sounded from the driveway. "Oh, that's Pete. Johnnie, Honey, go tell Pete I'll just be a couple more minutes." The boy didn't move. Nadine stamped her foot and spoke louder, "Don't just stand there, do as I say!" Johnnie turned and hurried outside to deliver the message. Nadine turned back to Claire and smiled.

Just them the baby started crying louder. "Claire, I'm desperate. I need your help."

Nadine dug into her purse, pulled out a crumpled paper and thrust it into Claire's hand. She then pushed the little girl away from her, quickly turned, put the baby on a chair and ran out the door just as Johnnie came in. He stood staring out the front door until a car door slammed shut. Gravel pinged about as the car sped away. He turned to Claire with a pitiful sad look on his face.

No one seemed to know what to do. "Please, miss, I'm hungry. Do you have a piece of bread I could have?" Claire felt a little hand touching hers. She looked down into the most beautiful green eyes, she had ever seen. They were surrounded by very dirty, brown, curly hair.

"Miss Claire? I think the baby is hungry, too." Claire looked over to where Nadine had laid the baby. Ann was now holding a tiny sickly-looking infant trying to sooth him. He was whimpering, not crying lustfully as one would expect.

"What's going on here? Where did these kids come from?" Claire looked up to the second-floor landing. Standing at the top of the stairs was her younger sister, Cecilia. Long, tasseled, ash blonde hair hung about her beautiful face which would have been stunning but for her vanity. Cecilia was thirteen going on twenty-one. Claire had been her surrogate mother since the death of their mother in influenza epidemic of 1918.

Claire knew her mother did not want another baby after the birth of her brother Preston. Just after Cecilia was born, Claire had overheard her mother telling a friend, "After I gave Anthony a son, I'd hoped that he would be satisfied and there would be no more pregnancies."

Continuing to gaze at the little girl, Claire sighed, "I'm not sure yet, what's going on." She turned to Ann, "Let's go downstairs and feed these children." Ann led the way, carrying the baby. Claire, holding the little girl's hand went next. Mr. Pierce smiled at Johnnie and beckoned him to join the parade. Cecilia came down the stairs and followed as she muttered, "What in the world is going on?"

As Claire followed Ann down the servants' stairs, she once again wondered why her mother had to be one of the people to have died. Things could have been so much easier. Instead, they ate with the servants in the basement. Father didn't even care.

He took many of his meals in his office while working. She knew her friends often made fun of her for eating with the help.

The butler and a maid had also succumbed to the influenza at the same time as Mother. The housekeeper was so upset and scared that she quit. Father failed to replace any of them. He had told Claire she was now in charge of the house. Claire was only a sophomore in high school. Trying to run the house and look after her brother and two sisters proved to be too much of a burden. She quit school midway through her junior year.

Claire was relieved to see Mrs. Wingate, the cook, up and making cocoa. She had slices of bread, butter and sugar sitting on the table. The other maid, Lily Lamont was also up and getting plates out of a cupboard. The baby continued to whimper.

Mrs. Wingate took the plates. "Lily, dilute some canned milk and heat it for the baby. I'll finish setting the table. Then perhaps someone can tell me what is going on and who are these children?"

Mrs. Wingate poured each person a cup of cocoa, including herself and both maids. She then sat in her usual chair at the end, or was it the head, of the table and began buttering and sprinkling sugar on the bread. When Mr. Pierce ate with the family, he always sat at the other end.

Johnnie produced a baby bottle from some place. The adults watched as he went to the stove and filled the bottle with the warm milk. He did not say a word but took the bottle and handed it to Ann then sat back down. Only after he had seen to the baby and his sister did he begin to eat. Mr. Pierce explained what he could.

"I heard awful pounding at the front door. I barely got the door open when Nadine pushed her way in. She seemed very agitated and was rambling on about Claire had to take the children. She said Claire was the only one that she trusted with them. At first, I wasn't even sure who the woman was. Then Claire came down and Nadine ran away."

Everyone sat drinking cocoa and eating bread except Claire. She straightened out the paper that had been given to her by Nadine. "Father, look at this."

Mr. Pierce took the wrinkled sheet Claire handed to him and read through it. "What is it?" asked Cecilia.

"It's a signed and witnessed document giving Claire custody of the children."

Claire froze, "Can someone just do that?"

"I really don't know. Tomorrow, or rather later today, I'll ask the company lawyer." Mr. Pierce looked down the table at the little girl, "Cecilia! Catch her!"

The child had fallen asleep and was about to topple onto the floor. Cecilia grabbed the girl and put the child on her lap.

Mr. Pierce checked the kitchen clock, which could be seen from the eating room. "It's 3:30. Let's go back to bed for a while. Claire, figure out where these children can sleep." Without saying more, Mr. Pierce got up and went to his room.

Claire was rightly miffed. This was her father's way. He was always leaving, expecting her to get things done.

"Lily, go to that back storage room. I think the old bassinet is in there. I'll get some blankets. Ann, would you mind if the baby stayed in your room for the night? It will be easier than dragging the bed up two flights of stairs." Ann nodded. Claire knew Ann had experience caring for children.

As Claire gathered the needed items, she recalled the day Ann had shown up at the kitchen door. She had known of Ann's family all her life, although not personally. They were poverty-stricken with several children. A friend had once told Claire that when a child in the family turned fourteen, he or she was told to find employment and take care of themselves.

That day a young kitchen helper found Claire and told her Mrs. Wingate requested she come to the kitchen. Ann was sitting on a stool hungrily eating bread smeared with a large portion of strawberry jam. Ann had heard about a maid having quit and came asking for the position. She was immediately hired.

Having picked up several linens, Claire returned to the eating room. "Come on, Cecilia, bring Johnnie with you." Claire looked at the boy, "That's your name, isn't it? That's what I heard your mother call you." Johnnie gave a drowsy nod. Claire led the way. Johnnie followed with Cecilia carrying the girl.

Once everyone had been settled, Claire returned to her room, took off her robe and slippers and turned out the light. Though, comfy in bed, sleep eluded her. She laid on her back staring at the ceiling. What in the world was she supposed to do? Could a woman just drop off her children and expect someone else to take them? And what about that poor baby? He behaved as though he were sick. She lay in bed what seemed like for hours, her mind a whirl of thoughts. Tomorrow was going to be difficult. Her mother told her when she had trouble going to sleep, she should either pray the Lord's prayer or repeat the twenty-third Psalm. Claire closed her eyes, "Our Father who art in heaven……." Before Claire was half way through the prayer, she was sound asleep.

Chapter 2

Claire woke and looked at the bedside clock. It was almost 10:00 a.m. When has she ever slept so late? She quickly dressed. On her way downstairs, she peeked into the guest's bedroom. The little girl was still asleep. The other bed was empty. She hurried downstairs.

Father's office was to the left of the stairs. The door was open so she walked in. He was not there. A door connected his office and his bedroom. This door was also open. Claire peeked in. The bed was made and the room unoccupied.

She crossed the marble floor of the foyer to the large living room. Her mother had make decorating this room her pet project, covering the walls with wheat-colored silk paper and the ceiling in a pleasing contrast of light buff. A large oriental rug covered the dark walnut floor. The eyes of everyone who stepped into the room were drawn to the white marble fireplace topped with a gilded mirror. Claire absently ran a finger over the wedding gift her father had given her mother so long ago, a pink porcelain clock with a multitude of bright pink and blue flowers. Memories of happy times when this room and the dining room daily hosted her family called to her to pause and sit on an overstuffed chair. But as she did, she heard voices coming up from below. Claire hurried down the back stairs.

"Good morning, Deary. Breakfast is on the table. I'll bring you a cup of coffee."

Faithful Mrs. Wingate, thought Claire. Always cheerful no matter what. Jewel Wingate had come to the Pierce home six months after the death of Mother. She had taken such splendid command of the kitchen that Claire had danced around the table.

Mrs. Wingate brought the promised coffee and she sat down in her usual seat. "Mrs. Wingate, we need to talk. Are Ann and Lily up yet?"

"Are they up! Goodness, gracious, Ann has been up with that baby most of what was left of the night. He has a bad tummy. The canned milk doesn't agree with him. Lily is out in the garden. She and the boy are picking strawberries."

A chafing dish of oatmeal was keeping warm over a candle. Mrs. Wingate pushed a plate of toast toward Claire. Claire fixed herself a small bowl of oatmeal and took a slice of toast. This had been the daily breakfast staple since Mother had died. The only exception was one Sunday morning each month. Those mornings Father cooked eggs, bacon and pancakes for his family and staff.

Claire swallowed, "Have Trudy and Olivia been down?" Olivia was Trudy's nurse. Trudy, the sister born three years after Claire, was "different." Her parents had refused to have any testing done on her. When she was old enough to go to school, her mother told the authorities, Trudy was being tutored at home. Claire was the one doing the tutoring.

Bright-eyed Trudy had never learned to print more than her name, yet she always seemed to be happy. That was until she was five. Claire remembered the day it had happened.

Claire had pieced together what she thought had changed her sweet sister based on what the child could relate and what others stated they were doing at the time.

Trudy had awakened from a nap to a quiet house. No one seemed to be around. Then she heard voices out the window. She climbed out of her crib and noticed three boys in an apple tree. That looked like fun to her. She put on her shoes and tiptoed down the back stairs. After a peek in the basement to find the cook sleeping in her rocking chair, she slipped past the maids' rooms ignoring the laughter coming from one of the rooms. She quietly strolled outdoors and to the orchard.

There were no limbs low enough for Trudy to reach. The industrious little girl saw a bench against the garden shed and dragged it to the tree. The bench made it possible for her to reach a limb. She continued to climb looking for just the right apple. She saw a large red one out at the end of a branch. Moving at a snail's pace, she made her way closer to the apple. Suddenly she heard the branch snap. Trudy, the apple, and the branch went down. The last thing she remembered was a pain shooting through her head.

The doctor did not give Trudy much hope for her survival. He cautioned her parents, "If Trudy lives, she may have permanent brain damage."

That was when the blaming started. Mother had not been home at the time of the accident. She had been out visiting a sister. Father shouted at her, saying she should have been home watching her children. Mother blamed Claire. She had expected Claire to be home by the time Trudy awoke from her nap. Claire didn't remember being told she was expected to be home to watch her sibling. She had stopped at a friend's house to see a litter of newborn kittens.

Trudy regained consciousness several weeks after the fall. She was a changed little girl. No longer was she the happy outgoing child she had once been. She became very self-centered with wide mood swings. A change in her routine resulted in anger. She would often lash out, hitting people and throwing objects for no apparent reason.

The only activity Trudy truly enjoyed was playing the piano. Although she could not read music, Claire had been able to teach her several simple songs which Trudy had memorized.

Claire loved Trudy yet resented her, which only added to her inability to forgive herself. Trudy was hot tempered, very mean and at times disagreeable. She was also devious. She took other people's belongings and hid them. More than once, when Claire had still been going to school, she hadn't been able to find her homework because Trudy had hidden it.

"Claire, did you hear what I said?" Claire turned to the cook. "You've been staring at the sugar bowl for five minutes. I thought you had gone to sleep."

"I'm sorry, Mrs. Wingate. What did you say?"

Mrs. Wingate repeated herself, "Nurse Olivia came down at seven. I was just starting breakfast. She asked what was going on. When I told her about the children, she said she'd take Trudy's breakfast up to their rooms."

Trudy did not take change well. When Mrs. Pierce died, Claire insisted Father hire a nurse for Trudy. Claire at the age of fifteen did not have the necessary experience to manage Trudy, Cecilia, her brother Preston, and undertake the housekeeper's duties.

There had been a succession of nurses until finally, Olivia came. One nurse had only stayed half a day before quitting. Olivia Watson had now been employed there for six years. She had been a nurse in the Great War and worked with shell-shocked soldiers. She usually knew exactly what to do when Trudy had one of her episodes. Claire thanked God every day for Olivia.

Mrs. Wingate poured herself a cup of coffee and sat down. She added a generous amount of cream and two teaspoons of sugar. She had to be tired. "I'm sorry, Mrs. Wingate," Claire said.

"You're sorry? What do you have to be sorry about? Is it your fault some woman shows up in the middle of the night and drops her babies in your lap?" The women heard crying coming from Ann's room. At the same time the back door opened and Johnnie and Lily came in carrying a basket of strawberries. "Well, look at those. Here, give them to me and I'll wash them. They'll be good in the oatmeal."

Claire watched as Johnnie gave the bowl to Mrs. Wingate. Turning to look at the little boy she asked, "Johnnie what are your sister's and brother's names? Here," she patted the seat beside her, "come and sit by me."

Johnnie did as he was told. Claire bent her head towards him and looked kindly into his big brown eyes. Finally, he spoke up, "My sister is Eva Taft and the baby is Adrian Taft. I'm Johnnie Rainy. We have different last names 'cause my daddy got killed in the war."

Once Johnnie started talking, it seemed he couldn't stop telling all that was bottled up in him. "I don't know what happened to Eva's daddy. We've lived with Peter Jacobson since Adrian was born. He doesn't like me or my sister and brother. He's mean to Mommie, too. Sometimes he hits her and yells when the baby cries. Eva and I hide when he gets mad." Then he began to cry.

Claire put her arm around him, "It's going to be okay. No one will hurt you or your sister or brother here."

Ann came into the room holding a crying Adrian. "Miss, I think there is something wrong with this baby. He cries all the time and doesn't seem to be able to eat. When he does eat, it comes flying back up."

Claire pushed her chair away from the table and walked over to Ann, "Give me the baby." As Ann handed Adrian to her, he vomited sour smelling, curdled milk over the front of Ann's dress. "Well, that doesn't look normal. Go change and I'll call Dr. Fletcher and ask if he will see the baby today. For now, we can try a little warm water and add a bit of syrup. Maybe it's just that the canned milk doesn't agree with him."

Cecilia came walking into the room holding Eva's hand. Eva's face was red from crying. She saw Johnnie, ran to him, and climbed onto his lap, almost knocking him off the chair. "Johnnie, I was scared. I didn't know where you were."

Cecilia plunked herself down in a chair with an exasperated sigh giving Claire a scornful look. "She was standing in the hall bawling her eyes out! Couldn't you hear her?"

 A little too loudly, Claire replied, "If we could have heard her, someone would have gone up to get her!" Apologetically, she added, "I'm sorry! Please go to the sink, get a towel, and wipe Eva's face. Eva, do you like strawberries?"

Eva squinted her eyes, "How do you know my name?"

"Johnnie told me. Can you tell me how old you are?" Eva held up three fingers. "Three! My goodness you're almost a young lady. Eva, do you know when your birthday is?" Eva hung her head shaking it.

Johnnie volunteered the answer. "It's in October, just before mine."

"And when is yours?"

Johnnie hesitated before answering, "Halloween."

Eva spoke up, "Uncle Peter makes fun of him for being born on Halloween. He called Johnnie a pumpkin. That's not nice, is it?"

"No, it isn't. We don't choose the day we are born." Claire returned to the subject of strawberries. "So, Eva, do you like strawberries?"

"I never had any."

"Oh, are you in for a treat! Mrs. Wingate, Eva and Johnnie must have some strawberries!"

The sweetened water wasn't any more successful staying down than the milk had been. Adrian was lethargic and warm. Claire walked out into the hall motioning for Cecilia to follow her. "I'm worried about this baby. I'm taking him upstairs to have Olivia look at him. You'll have to look after Johnnie and Eva."

"Me! I already have plans for today. Can't Ann or Lily babysit?"

"Ann has been up all night with Adrian. I told her to take the day off. Lily will have enough to do." Having said this, Claire started up the stairs.

"Well, it just isn't fair."

Claire stopped and turned half way around to face Cecelia, "Life isn't fair. You'd best realize that."

⌘

Olivia examined a protesting Adrian. She told Claire to feed him while she watched and felt his abdomen. "This child needs to be seen by a physician. You should take him to the emergency room. He's very sick. I think he might have a condition called 'pyloric stenosis.' If it is not treated now, he will most likely die."

Claire was dumbfounded. She carried the complaining infant to her room and rang for Ann. She explained to Ann what Olivia had said. Ann got the baby cleaned up as Claire put on more suitable clothes. Claire then went to the garage to get her car. Ann returned to the lower level to inform the others about the situation. Before Ann left to go with Claire, she told Cecelia that Claire wanted her to call Dr. Fletcher and Mr. Pierce about the situation.

When Father had decided not to replace the staff that had quit or died, he also considered letting the chauffeur, Arnold Cole go. That was until Claire asked how they were to get around as no one in the family knew how to drive. So, Arnold stayed. When they were old enough, Claire and her brother, Preston asked, Arnold to teach them to drive. Now both Claire and Preston had their own cars.

Dr. Fletcher came to the emergency examination room soon after Claire arrived. After examining the baby, he explained, "This infant has a condition called pyloric stenosis. It is an illness where the muscle between the stomach and small intestine is too thick and narrows the passageway. Little nourishment can pass through the opening. That's why he is having projectile vomiting and is restless. I'm sure he has lost some of his birth weight and for sure he has a chemical imbalance. If left untreated, he will probably die. He should have immediate surgery."

Claire signed the surgical and financial responsibility papers. Dr. Fletcher knew Claire was not the mother. She explained the situation.

He said, "What did you say the mother's name is?" When she repeated the name, he gave a knowing look at the nurse.

Surgery was scheduled for four that afternoon. A white gowned nurse picked up a whimpering Adrian and whisked him away. Another nurse gave Claire instructions as to where to wait. She said it would be better for her to leave and return nearer to four o'clock.

Claire and Ann were walking to the car when Father arrived in a cab. He got out and quickly paid the driver. "Father, I'm so glad to see you. Adrian is scheduled to have surgery at four this afternoon. Let's go someplace to eat. I'll explain what Dr. Fletcher said."

Claire drove the three of them to a nearby restaurant. Over lunch Claire described the problem with Adrian. She also explained what she had learned from Johnnie and Eva. After lunch it was decided that Ann should take a cab back to the house. "Please rest. Don't concern yourself about getting any work done. Tell Lily and Mrs. Wingate to rest, also. I'll call Vick's Restaurant and have supper brought to you." Ann appreciated Claire's thoughtfulness.

Mr. Pierce and Claire sat down on a park bench. Both were quiet for several minutes. Then Claire said, "What a night and a day this has been. Have you found out anything about Nadine and the man she was with? I don't think it was her husband."

Mr. Pierce didn't respond at first. Then he looked at Claire and said, "I take it you haven't had the radio on today."

Claire shook her head, "I should say not. I've hardly had time to think. Why?"

Mr. Pierce hesitated before saying more.

"Father, what is it?"

"Peter Jacobson, the man Nadine was with, tried to beat a train after they left

us. He didn't make it. Both were killed,
instantly."

Chapter 3

How does one tell a little girl and boy their mother is dead? Mrs. Wingate was cleaning up the supper dishes as Claire entered the kitchen.

"How did it go today? You look beat, child," Mrs. Wingate uttered.

"Mrs. Wingate, please get us some coffee and come sit with me." Mrs. Wingate brought each of them a cup and sat down. "Mrs. Wingate, Nadine is dead. She was killed in a car train accident just after they left here this morning."

"No! No!" Neither woman had noticed that Johnnie had come into the room. He stood frozen in the doorway.

"Oh Johnnie. I'm so sorry. I didn't see you there. Come over here." Johnnie walked slowly towards Claire. He stopped in front of her, almost touching her knees.

Very quietly he uttered, "It's not true. Please tell me it's not true."

She took him in her arms holding him tight. "It is true, Johnnie. I'm sorry, I'm so sorry." Johnnie cried uncontrollably. Claire looked to Mrs. Wingate for help.

Mrs. Wingate took Johnnie's hand and softly prayed. "Our heavenly Father, please help this little boy. Give the comfort that only You can give. Help him to endure this awful tragedy. And help him to be a comfort to his little sister. We ask this in Your holy name. Amen"

Nothing was said for several seconds. Finally, Johnnie raised his head and looked at Claire. "I must be brave for Eva. She won't understand."

"Yes, Johnnie, we all will. But we will be brave together and with Jesus's help we will get through this. Here, sit on my lap and Mrs. Wingate will get you some milk and cookies before we tell Eva."

As Johnnie had predicted, Eva did not understand. She kept asking when Mommie was coming back.

Father knew Nadine had a sister. His lawyer was able to locate her in a small village in upper New York state. She said her mother was living in an old people's home. Neither one had money to bury Nadine. Anthony Pierce saw no alternative but to pay for Nadine's funeral. He also paid train fare for Nadine's sister, Janice, to come to the funeral. The mother was physically unable to travel.

A gentle rain had fallen most of the night before Nadine's funeral. By early morning high winds had driven away the rain clouds. Father and Claire sat at the breakfast table debating rather or not Eva should attend the funeral. Nurse Olivia overheard their conversation as she came down to get a breakfast tray for Trudy and herself. Not surprisingly, she spoke up. "I think she should be allowed to attend. She should see her mother in the casket. It will help her to understand what has happened."

"She's only three! When Momma died, Preston was seven and he still couldn't comprehend why Momma was in a box. He talked about it endlessly."

"Claire, I think Olivia is right," Father volunteered. "The child may not totally understand but it will help her face the finality of death."

 Claire looked at her father rather than Olivia. She kept her mouth closed as she gritted her teeth. How dare she? Olivia hadn't been present when Mrs. Pierce had died and didn't know what Claire had gone through. She had been mourning her mother's death while trying to cope with Preston and Cecilia's grief. Her father had kept himself in his office during most of this time. He hadn't been present to deal with Cecilia's constant crying and questioning.

Three days later, Rev. Cameron Forester presided at Nadine's funeral. He had only recently been ordained. This was his first time conducting a funeral. His nervous manner was plain to all.

Claire was surprised at the number of people attending the service. There were a goodly number she didn't know. She thought, possibly, they were Father's associates.

At the conclusion of the service, the funeral director started to close the lid on the casket in preparation for the removal to the cemetery. Eva stood up on the pew and shrieked, "No! Don't close the door. Mommie won't be able to breathe."

Preston had driven in from college to attend the funeral. He was sitting behind Eva. He lifted Eva, and carried the screaming child out of the church. Johnnie quietly followed behind them. Claire was devastated.

A luncheon was served at the family home after the interment. Mr. Pierce approached Nadine's sister, Janice. He asked if she planned to take the children.

 Wide eyed and in a voice loud enough for all to hear, Janice declared, "I have five children of my own. I cannot afford and do not want Nadine's kids. It's perfectly agreeable to me to let these brats stay with you."

When questioned about the where-abouts of Eva's and Adrian's father, she stated," I have no idea. All I know is that Pete Jacobson is not their father. Last time I got a letter from Nadine, she was five months along with Adrian. Nadine told me she had left her husband, Jasper Taft, and was living with Jacobson."

Mr. Pierce refused to pay for Pete Jacobson's burial. The police tracked down Jacobson's mother. She said she had no money. Jacobson was buried in a pauper's grave.

Chapter 4

Three days after the funeral, Robert came to call.

Robert Collins was Claire's fiancé. She did not love him. Why was she willing to marry a man she did not love? She recognized that this would probably be her last chance for marriage and a family of her own.

They had been engaged for over two years and twice Claire had postponed the wedding. She doubted he loved her since they had remained engaged, despite the postponements. If he truly loved her, wouldn't he push to be wed?

Instead, he habitually reminisced about serving as an Army officer in the Great War. He'd given his right leg at the Battle of St Michiel in France. His frequent melancholy and short—temperedness were other reasons she was in no hurry to marry him.

Many men had been killed in the Great War leaving a plethora of "unclaimed jewels" such as Claire. Still, she hesitated to marry someone she didn't love.

From time to time, Claire wondered why Robert wanted to marry her. Of course, he worked for her father, and after proposing he was given a promotion and a hefty pay raise. It raised the question; that she couldn't ask either her father or Robert for fear she already knew the answer.

So here he was, after skipping the funeral. Why hadn't he come sooner or at least called? Father must surely have told him.

Claire entered the living room followed by Ann carrying a tray with coffee and cakes. Robert gazed out a window watching the children playing. At the age of thirty-three, he was still handsome with dark brown eyes and dusky brown hair, though he was overly thin for his more than six-foot frame. Perhaps being a bachelor, he didn't eat well.

"Hello, Robert. Aren't the children lovely. Come sit down. Ann, you can leave. I'll pour the coffee."

"None for me. I don't feel like coffee." He kept his back to her still staring outside. "Is some relative of these kids going to take them?"

Robert's blunt statement startled Claire. He said nothing about the children's loss or what problems she might be experiencing. Well, she could be just as blunt. "What do you mean? Before Nadine died, she signed a paper giving me custody. Our family lawyer, Stanley Ferris, is looking into the matter. I hope to be granted permanent custody."

"You hope to get custody! What about me? You haven't asked me what I want."

The truth that she should have, stabbed at her. She never considered asking him. "You're right, Robert. I guess I just thought you would accept the situation and the children would be part of our family. I must add I was disappointed when you failed to visit or at least call me. You don't seem to care about what happened. Do you even understand what's going on?"

Robert turned from looking out the window. Placing his hands on his hips and leaning forward with a scowl on his face, Robert blared, "Yes, I understand. You bet I understand! As to you thinking I'd just accept these urchins, you're thinking wrong. I want nothing to do with them. I don't want to be stuck with some other man's brats!"

Claire rose. "They are not brats! They are children and they need us."

"They don't need me! What would you have done if we had already been married when this happened? The decision would have been up to me. It should still be up to me. If you want me to marry you, find another place for them."

Almost shouting, Claire responded, "I didn't ask you to marry me. You're the one that asked me to marry **you.**"

"You really don't know why I proposed?"

"I thought you cared for me and wanted me."

"Hah! It was your father. He wants you to get married. He promised me a promotion, a raise, and a house if I married you. I can't think of another reason why I'd marry you."

Claire was shocked. She dropped to the couch and studied Robert. Slowly she removed her engagement ring and held it out for him. He stood looking at it. "Give it to your father. He's the one who paid for it." He turned on his heels and left. The front door slam reverberated throughout the house.

With shaking hands Claire poured herself a cup of coffee, spilling some on the polished mahogany coffee table. She didn't want to think of Robert or how his words had cut her to ribbons. If she ever had feelings for the man, they were now gone.

Eventually Ann came into the room. "Is there anything I can do for you?"

"I suppose you heard?"

"Yes Miss, the doors were open."

"Please take the tray to the kitchen. I'll be in my room, if I'm needed." She would not throw herself on the bed and cry. She would not lament marrying Robert. He wasn't much of a loss.

However, her father was another matter. Anger and hurt mingled as she reviewed her father's meddling. How could he do such a thing? He had sold her! The thought made her knees grow weak and she sat at her desk regaining her balance.

Out her window she spotted Lily playing with Johnnie and Eva.

And Rev. Forester!

Claire didn't know he had come. No one had said anything to her. The whole house probably heard Robert's voice, including the pastor. Oh, no!

She didn't feel up to pretending pleasantries with him.

Although it wasn't Lily's place to entertain the minister, she appeared to be handling the situation. The four, Lily, Rev. Forester, Johnnie, and Eva, were kicking a large rubber ball. Claire could see they were having a grand time. Eva missed her kick every time. She would laugh and run after it.

Claire sat back in her chair. When Father got home, she knew they had to have a talk. Perhaps postponing her wedding had been God directing her. From this day on, she determined, her goal would be to love and nurture these children.

When Father came home that evening, Claire knew instinctively who knocked on her door. "Come in, Father."

It was obvious that Anthony Pierce already knew about Robert telling Claire the circumstance regarding the engagement. She could read it on his face. He stood at the threshold slumped shouldered. His eyes were puffy and red. Had he been crying? Gazing at his daughter sorrowfully, he cautiously entered the room.

Neither father nor daughter said anything for what seemed like an eternity. At length he broke the silence, "Claire, I'm sorry. I'm so sorry. It was wrong for me to have pressured Robert into dating you."

"You sold me! You sold me for what? A better position, more pay, and a house!" Claire realized she was screaming. This made her upset even more. She took a deep breath before continuing. "Father, how could you have done such a dastardly, reprehensible, deceitful, and mean thing? You shamed me! How did you think you could do that? Did somebody make you God?"

"I only wanted you to be happy. I thought he was a good man. And this might be the last chance for you to get married and have a family of your own. I only meant it for your good."

Claire could see the grief and regret in his eyes. Yet her anger made logic difficult. What was she to do? She walked to a window and stared. It had grown dark. What was the use?

To her surprise, she heard her father crying. She turned. There stood her gentle father with his hands over his face sobbing. She went to him and wrapped her arms around him.

Anthony wiped his face with his handkerchief. Gazing into her eyes he uttered, "If you can forgive me, I promise to do all I can to make you happy. I'll never interfere or manipulate your choices ever again."

Claire hugged her father. "It's over, Father. We must go on. We have other more serious matters to attend to."

"Yes, we do. May I sit?"

Claire took her father by his elbow and guided him to one of two upholstered chairs by her window. When had Father gotten so old? She sat in the other chair.

Father took a deep breath, then continued. "My company's lawyer, Stan Ferris came to visit me this afternoon. He's been trying to track down the children's birth certificates. The boy's was easy. He was born October 31, 1918. He'll be ten this year. His full name is John Nicholas Rainy. His father was Nicholas John. He died October 4, 1918." He handed Claire Johnnie's certificate.

She reviewed her father's words. "That was just a little more than a month before the war ended. How sad."

"Yes, you're right. This is Eva's certificate. Her name is Eva Hope Taft. Her birth date is October 15, 1924. Which will make her four this October." Claire reached her hand to receive the paper her father was holding out.

"Stan couldn't find Adrian's birth certificate. He figures it was probably a home birth and Nadine never got around to registering it."

Claire stared at her father wide eyed, "What does that mean? Did Mr. Ferris say what we should do?"

"He suggested we hire a private investigator. If he can learn where Nadine lived when she gave birth, hopefully there will be a witness. Maybe there was a lady that attended her and can remember the date. Then we can get her affidavit and have the birth registered. He also suggested we talk to Johnnie. He might know something."

"I'll have to think of some way to talk to him. I don't want to upset him."

Chapter 5

The occasion to learn about Adrian's birth presented itself in an unexpected way. The Pierce's white and tan collie dog, Roxy gave birth to three puppies. The children were in a storage room in the lower level looking at the puppies when Johnnie spoke, "I saw Adrian get born."

Claire was aghast, "You what?" She took a deep breath and motioned for Johnnie to come into the eating room. "Sit down and tell me about it." Claire sat in her father's chair. Johnnie sat next to her.

"Mommie was walking back and forth in the front room, crying, and holding her tummy. It was really big. She had been in bed most of the day. Uncle Peter yelled at her to be quiet. He put his coat on and said he was leaving. Mommie yelled at him to get a doctor. He said he would, but he never came back. I asked her if she would fix something for me and Eva to eat. She was crying and told me to go get Mrs. March."

"Who is Mrs. March?"

"She lived below us. I think she owns our building. Mommie was always promising to give her money for our rent. I went downstairs to get her but she wasn't home. So, I knocked on Mr. and Mrs. Calloway's door. They live next to Mrs. March. Their apartment is much nicer than ours. Mr. Calloway answered. I told him Mommie was sick and needed help. He said he would have Mrs. Calloway go up."

"I went back upstairs to our apartment. Mommie was still walking around holding her stomach and crying. Eva was crying too. I didn't know what to do. I was scared because her stomach was so big. She yelled at Eva to stop crying. That only made Eva cry more." Here Johnnie stopped and put his elbows on the table and his head in his hands.

Claire touched his arm, "You don't have to go on if you don't want to."

Johnnie looked up at Claire, "Could I have something to drink?"

"Of course. I'll be right back."

Mrs. Wingate must had been watching because before Claire got out of her chair. Cook came in with milk and a plate of cookies. Smiling she placed the glass and cookies near Johnnie. He took a long drink from the glass and shoved a whole cookie in his mouth.

Claire waited for him to finish chewing and swallow before motioning him to continue.

Johnnie sighed, "Mrs. Calloway finally came. So did Mrs. March. Mrs. March told me to take Eva across the hall to Mrs. Waller's apartment. She said for us to stay there and have Mrs. Waller bring over some sheets. Mrs. Waller is a real old lady. I had to knock and knock before she answered." Johnie stopped to take another drink and eat another cookie.

Claire did the best she could to be patient.

"Mrs. Waller turned the radio on and said to stay put. We didn't mind because we don't have a radio and I liked listening to it.

We could hear Mommie scream even with the radio on.

"Eva started crying again. I didn't know what to do. I held Eva until she fell asleep. Then I went back to our apartment. No one saw me. Everyone was in the kitchen.

"Mommie was laying on the table. She didn't have any clothes on. Mrs. Calloway was holding one leg up by her shoulder. Mrs. March had the other leg up the same way. I thought that strange. Mommie would have yelled at me if I got on the table like that. Mrs. Waller was doing something between Mommie's legs. Mrs. Waller kept saying, 'It's almost here. Push, push.'

"Then Mrs. Waller was holding Adrian. He was blue. She started slapping him and blowing in his face. He was naked too! Finally, he started crying and the ladies smiled and laughed. Then Mrs. Calloway saw me and yelled at me to go away. I went back to Mrs. Waller's apartment."

Having finished his story, Johnnie looked at Claire, "Was Adrian in Mommie's stomach?"

"Yes, he was. You saw him get born."

"How did he get in there? How did he get out?"

Claire wasn't sure what to say. Finally, she attempted a simple reply, "Well, it's very hard to explain. Sometimes when a husband and wife love each other a lot, God gives them a baby. It grows inside the Mommie until it is big enough to be born. Then God makes a way for the baby to come out."

"Did my daddy love my Mommie?"

"Yes, he loved her very much."

"Did Jasper love my Mommie?"

"Yes, he did."

"Then why did he leave?"

"That I don't know." Claire abruptly changed the subject, "Johnnie, do you know the address where you lived in that apartment?"

"No."

"Can you tell me anything about the apartment and other buildings around it?"

"It has three floors. We lived on the second one. Only Mr. Goodnight lived on the top floor. He had ladies come visit him. Mrs. March would get mad at him and tell him she was going to make him move if they didn't stop visiting him. Eva and I liked to watch the ladies. They were mostly pretty and dressed up in bright clothes." Johnnie stopped and gazed away as if he were remembering.

"Johnnie, can you tell me anything about what other buildings were on your street?"

"The Strand movie house was just three buildings away. Sometimes Mommie took Eva and me to the movies there. And across the street from our building was Andy's repair shop. I used to sneak over there to watch the men work on the cars."

"You've been very helpful. I think Eva is still playing with the puppies. Why don't you get her and go outside and swing? Please, don't make the swing go too high." On the back lawn was an ornate wooden swing with two seats facing each other.

Claire went upstairs and telephoned the investigative agency Father had employed.

The detective assigned to the case was a woman. This peeved Mr. Pierce and pleased Claire greatly.

A week later, Claire was sitting at her desk when she heard a car drive up. It was Miss Horme from the detective agency. Claire came down the stairs as Ann was helping Miss Horme off with her coat.

Miss Horme offered her hand to Claire. "Good afternoon, Miss Pierce. I have very good news for you."

"Please come into the parlor. May I offer you a cup of coffee or tea?"

"Tea if you please."

"Of course. Ann, ask Mrs. Wingate for tea and a tray of sweets." Please sit, Miss Horme, and tell me the good news."

"Well, I interviewed the three ladies that were present at Adrian's birth. We have signed and notarized statements from each one. They agreed that Adrian was born on May 6, 1928, at about eight in the evening."

"Oh, that's wonderful."

"Mrs. Waller even told me she asked Nadine who the father of the boy is. She said Jasper Taft was her husband and father of both Eva and Adrian."

Ann arrived with the tea and small cakes. The ladies took time to prepare their tea and sample the cakes.

"Do you have the papers with you?" Claire asked between bites of cake.

"No, I gave Mr. Ferris, your lawyer, the information, and he will be getting a birth certificate for Adrian. I understand

Adrian was not given a middle name. So, you or someone will have the honor of selecting one.

The new family settled into a routine. Adrian now slept in Claire's room. He grew so fast he seemed to only wear a garment two or three times before he had out grown it. Johnnie and Eva still shared a guest bedroom. Eva was Johnnie's shadow, ever present near him. They relished having Preston home for the summer. He could frequently be found playing in the yard with them, his good-natured laugh mingled with their giggles.

One day Claire heard him ask Johnnie, "What grade will you be in when school starts?"

Johnnie hung his head, saying nothing. "Johnnie, what's wrong?"

He gazed at Preston with his sad brown eyes, "I've never been to school. Mommie said I had to stay home and watch Eva while she worked."

Claire bit her tongue to keep from saying the wrong thing. "Well, you will be ten in October. I think that means you should probably be entering either the fourth or fifth grade. We'll just see what we can do to get you caught up."

Mrs. Wingate rang a bell to let everyone know lunch was ready. "Johnnie, you and Eva go ahead to lunch. Tell Mrs. Wingate Preston and I will be in later. Claire had an inspiration. She was thinking of a plan to teach Johnnie, and while she was at it to help Preston earn money. If her plan worked, he would not have to ask Father for money so often.

She knew Preston did not like having to ask their father every time he needed money. It was not that their father was a miser. He just seemed to have a blind spot about how to run a house and did not understand the needs of his children. Claire knew he was wealthy. Her father did not trust banks after her grandfather had lost a great deal of money in the panic of 1884.

"Ok, Sis. What did I do wrong now?"

Claire smirked. Was she really that transparent? "You haven't done anything wrong. Let's go sit on the swing. I have an idea." The two sat across from each other, the swing gently swaying.

"Johnnie needs to learn how to read and learn his numbers. I know you would like it if you didn't always have to ask Father for money."

"Boy, that's the truth. We're not paupers. I know Dad squirrels away money. I'll bet he has more money in safe deposit boxes, the safe in his office here at the house and the one in his office than Rockefeller. Besides all his stock certificates."

"Calm down, Preston. We're not as rich as Rockefeller. But, yes, you're right, we are far from destitute."

"Yeah! And I resent how Dad lets you have the combination to everything. I'm old enough to take some responsibility."

"You are so right. Now, please, listen to my plan."

"Okay, Sis, shout it out."

"I would like you to tutor Johnnie in reading and arithmetic. Even if he's not up to his grade level this fall, at least he will know something. In exchange you will get paid."

"Hold it right there. I don't know anything about teaching, and I don't intend to spend my summer in a classroom."

"Why don't you visit Miss Maxwell, the grade school principal?"

"That old witch!"

"Preston! Really."

"I spent more 'quality time' in her office than I care to remember. She'd laugh at me."

"Well, whose fault was that? You know you deserved everything you got. Please."

Preston sighed, "Okay, okay. Say I agree to do this, how much is it worth to you? And just how much time each day will this involve?"

Claire bit her bottom lip, "What would you say to ten dollars a week and to teaching from eight in the morning to twelve noon?"

"I'm worth more than that. I'd say fifty dollars a week and nine to noon with fifteen-minute breaks every hour."

"Preston! You know that is way out of the question. I think fifteen dollars is more than fair if you will tutor Johnnie from eight to twelve noon with ten-minute breaks."

Preston scowled at Claire, then sighed, "Twenty dollars, eight to twelve with fifteen-minute breaks."

Claire offered her hand, "Deal!" Then she hugged him. "Let's go tell Johnnie the good news."

Two days later Claire was playing patty-cake with Adrian and Eva. The front door opened and she heard Preston come in. He had been to the grade school to see Miss Maxwell. He walked into the parlor.

"Eva, go see Mrs. Wingate. Tell her I said you may have a cookie." Eva jumped up and flew out of the room. Claire regarded Preston. "What is it? You look glum."

Well, Miss Maxwell wants to test Johnnie. I just talked to him and he's refusing."

"Don't push him. He's been through so much. He still acts like he needs to protect Eva and Adrian. Just set up the tutoring around the dining room table and see what happens. I'll deal with Miss Maxwell."

Three days later Claire peeked in at the classroom. She was surprised to see Johnnie's shadow, Eva sitting with a book. Preston spied Claire, "Come on in, Sis. We're ready for a break."

"Eva, I'm surprised to see you here."

"I want to learn, too."

With a questioning gaze Claire studied Preston. Before she could say anything, Preston responded with a wink, "I'll tell you about it later."

Suddenly banging came from the unused butler's pantry. Preston sighed, "It's Trudy again! That's the third time today she's interfered with us."

"Let me handle her." Claire marched into the pantry. "**TRUDY!** Stop bothering Preston and the children!"

"I don't like them! And I don't want them here. This is my house."

As calmly as Claire was able to, she responded, "I know this is your house. It is also my house and everyone else who lives here. That includes the children. It is also a very big house. There are plenty of rooms you can go to where you will not be disturbed.

"I want to play the piano and it's in the living room. Preston said I can't because it bothers the kids."

"You can wait until this afternoon and play it then."

"**NO!** I don't want them here! Maybe they'll be sorry they ever came here." Having said that Trudy stamped her foot and marched away leaving a mess of pans, lids, and utensils in the middle of the floor.

Later that evening, Claire sought Preston out. To her surprise, he was sitting at the dining room table planning tomorrow's lesson. She smiled as she pulled out a chair across the table from him.

Preston eyed his sister. "This is really kind of fun. I may change my major and become a teacher. Were you surprised to see Eva with us?"

I was. If she's bothering you, I'll see that she has other things to do."

"No, she's okay. I think she's going to give Johnnie a run for his money. Johnnie's a good student. Eva is an excellent one. She's learning almost as much as

Johnnie. I had to get another set of books and tablets."

"Do you think Johnnie minds her presence?"

"If he does, he hasn't said anything. He struggles with reading but is quick with his numbers. Eva is sharp, grasping both. Both relish geography. I'm thinking of using *The National Geographic* for reading and geography. We could talk about the topics in the magazines and declare that someday we'll visit the far-off countries."

They heard Adrian start to cry. Claire sighed. "That baby has been fussy all day. He won't eat and has hardly slept. I think he might also be running a slight temperature."

"Maybe he's cutting a tooth. Rub his gums like you used to do for Cecilia."

"I'm surprised you remember that."

"I remember a lot of things you used to do, especially after Mom died. You've spent practically your whole life doing for us."

Claire smiled remembering those days, before responding to Preston. "Adrian's barely four months old. I think that's a little young to be cutting teeth. Well, I need to go." Unenthusiastically she got up.

Finally, just after eleven Adrian, exhausted, fell into a restless sleep.

Chapter 6

Something woke Claire. At first, she thought it was Adrian. As she rolled to her side, she saw Trudy standing over the crib holding a knife. "No, Trudy! No!" Claire jumped out of bed and lunged for Trudy.

"Let me go. I don't want him here!" Trudy brought the knife down slicing Claire's arm. Blood sprayed across both women and Adrian.

Claire ignored the pain as she tried to restrain Trudy. She began shouting, "Help me! Preston, I need help!" Adrian was now awake and crying. She couldn't believe

Trudy's strength. It was incredible. Claire yelled again, "Preston, someone, it's Trudy, she has a knife. I can't hold her off. She's trying to hurt Adrian."

Strong hands grabbed hold of Trudy and wrestled her to the floor. "Let me go! Let me go! I don't want them here."

The bedroom light came on. Claire saw Preston and Trudy struggling on the floor. Cecilia came over to Claire and helped her to a chair.

Claire watched dazed. She felt something being pressed against her arm. Cecilia was putting pressure on it using a pillow, trying to stem the blood flow.

Adrian was crying piercingly. Johnnie awakened by his crying and Claire's shouting ran into the room. He dashed to his brother's crib and picked him up. "It's okay, baby. I'm here. I won't let anything happen to you." Holding his brother, he moved to the side of the room and examined Adrian. Satisfied the blood wasn't Adrian's, he held him tight trying to comfort his frightened brother.

The struggle between Trudy and Preston continued about the floor. They knocked over a small table. The objects resting on it were propelled across the room. A blue delph ware lamp, a favorite gift from Claire's mother, was shattered as it crashed against the brick fireplace.

Olivia entered the room holding a hypodermic syringe. "Hold her down, Preston, so I can give her a shot."

Preston chanced a look at Olivia, "What do you think I've been trying to do?" He finally managed to turn Trudy to her stomach and sat on her back holding her arms out. She continued to violently kick, hitting Preston in his back several times. Olivia gave Trudy the injection. After less than a minute, Trudy relaxed. Preston got off his sister and sat on the floor with his arms wrapped around his legs and his head resting on his knees. "Man! Is she strong!"

Olivia went over to Claire to see about her cut. "This is bad. You need to go to the emergency room for stitches."

"No, please just clean it up and wrap a dressing around it. I'll go in the morning."

"You'll do no such thing!" Father had entered the room. Preston, carry Trudy to her room and tie her down!"

Olivia shot Mr. Pierce a disturbed look, "That's not necessary. The medication will knock her out for several hours."

"Olivia, I don't care. Preston, do as I say."

Ann, Lily, and Mrs. Wingate had heard the commotion from their rooms in the lower level. Mr. Pierce noticed them standing in the hall. "Lily, go wake up Arnold and have him bring the car around. Ann, help Claire into something decent to wear to the hospital." Adrian was crying loudly. "Mrs. Wingate, take the baby. Make sure he isn't hurt. I'm going to get dressed. Ann, you come with us to the hospital." Each person hastily moved to do as instructed.

Shattered, Claire was helped into the hospital lobby by Father. An attendant brought a wheel chair. "Sir, you will have to wait out here."

"I'll do nothing of the sort! I'm going back with her."

The evening had been a particular busy and trying period. The attendant sighed and shrugged his shoulders, "Follow me." Ann obediently remained seated in the waiting room.

Claire was helped onto a narrow bed. Father surveyed the E.R. Now there were only two other people waiting treatment. One was a drunk with a broken arm. The other person had hiccups since yesterday. Why did he choose now at midnight to seek help?

Claire sat staring about the room. What were they going to do about Trudy? A nurse came in and smiled, "Hello, I'm Miss Tidwell." As she was speaking, she pulled a curtain around the bed. "I'm going to give you a shot that will ease your pain before the doctor sutures the wound." After giving the injection, she promptly hurried out.

Father sat on a chair in the corner, "What is all that racket?"

Claire peered between an opening where the nurse had failed to close the curtain all the way. The drunk, now totally nude, was meandering around the room knocking equipment over. Claire realized this was the first time she had ever seen a completely naked grown man! "My!"

Two hospital attendants quickly seized the gentleman and escorted him back to his bed. Father got out of his chair and hastily secured the opening. "Really, Claire!" Claire smirked.

A curtain separated Claire's bed from the hiccupping man's bed. She could hear someone, probably a doctor, giving words of advice to this patient.

Her curtain was pulled back by Nurse Tidwell carrying a tray with an assortment of articles. "I'm going to clean your wound. It may hurt some. The shot I gave you should help alleviate the pain some."

The medicine hadn't had time to work. Claire instinctively pulled back her arm and yelped.

"See here Nurse!" Father protested. "You just gave her the shot. It hasn't had time to work."

"Mr. Pierce, please sit down and be quiet, or I'll have to ask you to leave."

"It's okay, Father. I shouldn't have yelled." Claire lay back and endured the procedure.

Just as Nurse Tidwell finished, a very handsome young man entered the area. He was not tall but his black hair and dark penetrating eyes were gorgeous. He was followed by an older distinguished looking, silver haired woman. Both wore white coats. The lady offered her hand to Father. "Good morning, I'm Doctor Fisher and this is Doctor Eisner." Father and Doctor Fisher shook hands. Claire lay on the bed like a child.

After washing their hands, the physicians donned rubber gloves. "Doctor Eisner is an intern and will be doing the procedure. I will assist," explained Dr. Fisher.

Father shot up from his chair, "You mean, he's just learning how to be a doctor?"

"No, no. Doctor Eisner is a certified physician. He's doing his internship here before opening his own practice." Doctor Eisner flashed a comforting smile at Claire.

Doctor Eisner expertly applied his skill. Claire gritted her teeth and focused on the green curtain. The injection still had not taken effect. She didn't want to say anything for fear her father would make a scene.

Before the doctors were finished, a second nurse came in, "Dr. Fisher, a child has arrived with breathing difficulty." Doctor Fisher left. Dr. Eisner hurriedly finished and left as soon as the last suture was in.

Nurse Tidwell began bandaging Claire's arm. "I'm sorry if the doctors' actions seem abrupt. They've been on duty for sixteen hours. Until just before you arrived, the place was packed. No one has had time for more than short coffee breaks. Leave your arm bandaged, and wear this sling. Make an appointment to see your own physician in a couple of days." Having finished her little speech, she called an attendant to take Claire to her car.

Chapter 7

It was after four o'clock in the morning when their car drove down the lane to the house. The pain injection had finally taken effect. "Mr. Pierce, Claire is asleep." Ann and Claire were in the back seat.

Mr. Pierce was in the front with Arnold. He turned to see Claire sleeping on Ann's shoulder. "Arnold, drive to the back door." The car continued down the gravel drive toward the kitchen walkway.

The house was built on a slight regress. The lower level at the rear of the house was only five steps below ground level.

Anthony Pierce got out of the car and fleetingly viewed the land between the house and woods that was bathed in first light. When his wife was living, the ground included several areas of various flower plots. Claire had managed to keep a small rose garden, which she affectionately tended. Anthony's heart ached for what was lost, for what might have been.

"Claire, wake up, we're home. Arnold, come help me with Claire," Father directed. Claire could not stand on her own.

Arnold, a strong hurly man, picked her up and carried her down the stairs. "I'll carry her to her room if you'll show me the way."

"Her room hasn't been cleaned yet." Mrs. Wingate said this as she came into the hall from the kitchen. "Put her in my room. We can keep a better eye on her down here." Arnold tenderly laid Claire on Mrs.

Wingate's bed and covered her with a quilt. He discreetly left the room.

"Mrs. Wingate, have you not been back to bed?" asked Mr. Pierce.

"I fed the baby then dozed some. Don't worry about me. Old people don't need as much sleep as you youngsters." In truth Mrs. Wingate was two years younger than Anthony Pierce, fifty-three.

"Arnold, I won't be going into work today." Anthony Pierce looked at the staff standing in the hall. "Please, just take it easy today. Do what is only necessary." Having said this, Pierce poured himself a cup of coffee from the pot Mrs. Wingate always seemed to have ready. He walked into the eating room and sat down.

He was wiped out. If he could go back to bed, he would have. But he knew decisions had to be made. Mrs. Wingate followed him with her own cup of coffee. "I don't know what to do. I can't let this happen again. Mrs. Wingate, do you have any suggestions?"

"As a matter-of fact, I do. It's not going to be cheap, however."

"Money, we have. Tell me your thoughts?"

"First, you'll need a pad and pencil." Mrs. Wingate said this as she rummaged through a buffet drawer. She handed her employer the items and sat down.

Anthony looked perplexingly at the pad and pencil, "You have so many ideas that I'll need these?"

"Yes, I do." She used her fingers to tick off her thoughts. "One, I think Trudy and Olivia should move to the doll house."

The doll house was actually a very large two-story stone house at the north edge of the property. Anthony's parents had decided to give their son and daughter-in-law the family home. They had the stone house built for them to live in.

Mrs. Wingate continued, "I don't know what condition the place is in, having not been used for seven years. But I imagine it wouldn't take much to get it livable. You'll also have to hire a cook and housekeeper for them."

"I'm not sure Trudy would like to move there. You know how she dislikes change."

"Sir, she sure doesn't like the changes here. I think if handled properly, she can adjust to the idea. And I'm sure Olivia will enjoy having a place she can call her own. She isn't real pleased, right now, either."

Anthony looked discouragingly across the table, but wrote down the suggestion. "What's next?"

"Number two." Mrs. Wingate bent down each finger as she expressed her ideas. "When was the last time you were in your wife's apartment?"

Anthony appeared shocked and regarded Mrs. Wingate several seconds. "I haven't been in her rooms in years. Why"

"If you had been, you would know the place is falling apart. The glue from that expensive hand painted wallpaper is loosening. Several strips of paper are hanging almost to the floor. The beautiful lace curtains she waited so many months to arrive from Holland are mostly rotted. The carpet is sun faded."

"What is your point?"

"Let Claire and the baby move into the apartment. One of the rooms can be a nursery and the other one Claire's bedroom. Mind you, you'll have to provide money for her to redecorate the place."

Sighing, he wrote on the pad then turned his attention back to the cook, "I take it you have more?"

"I still have three fingers." She smiled as she said this. "Three, move Johnnie and Eva into Trudy's and Olivia's apartment. Each will have their own bedroom and still not be too far from one another. The present sitting room can be a play room."

"What's wrong with the ballroom? That's a whole floor of play room?"

Anthony Pierce's grandparents had enjoyed entertaining and having parties. The third floor was designed to be a ballroom. There were country scenes on the walls, with an oak dance floor and crystal chandeliers. French doors opened onto a large balcony. There were even two bathrooms and a coat room. Neither Anthony or his wife had cared much for dancing or parties. The children were allowed to use the ballroom as a playroom.

"Just when was the last time you were up there?" Anthony only pursed his lips and sighed. Mrs. Wingate continued, "I thought so. If you had taken the time to check out the place, you would know rain has leaked through the roof unto the attic floor and down through the ceiling to the third floor. A good part of that lovely dance floor is ruined. The toys are mostly broken. As for the chandeliers, Preston used them as targets when playing with his BB gun."

"Why didn't Claire tell me about the bad roof?"

"Don't you be blaming Claire for something you should have been looking after!"

Anthony hung his head, "You're right of course. What else needs to be done?"

"Look around you. This is not a proper place for a family of your position to be eating. The family should be eating upstairs in the formal dining room. Not down here in a basement. And while we're at it, that kitchen is like working in a dungeon. The butler's pantry, next to the dining room, could be made into a lovely modern kitchen."

Anthony had been writing as Mrs. Wingate clicked off her suggestions on her fingers. "You haven't used all your fingers yet. Is there more?"

Mrs. Wingate regarded her fingers, spreading them wide in front of her. Then she intertwined them and rested them on the table. "Yes, there are just a couple of things that could use attention. The last time Ann's and Lily's rooms had anything done to them was several years before Mrs. Pierce passed. I think the old housekeeper, Mrs. Cromford, was still here. The mattresses in those rooms are very thin. The windows let in cold air, and Lily's dresser is propped up with a book."

Giving another long sigh, Anthony placed his pencil next to the pad and gazed about the room. "You know, you're right. Let's have a family meeting, including the staff, tonight after supper. We'll go through this list."

"Don't you think it would behoove you to talk with Claire, alone, first."

"Of course, you're right, again."

Anthony was rather relieved that Mrs. Wingate had brought this up. He knew things had to change, but he was too tired to think after all the excitement and worry concerning his daughters. He was a very good business man. As to home business, he had left those first to his wife, now to Claire.

Mr. Pierce and the cook sat in comfortable silence, each with his and her own thoughts.

Ann came down the stairs followed by a tall man. "Mr. Pierce, this is police officer, Lieutenant Dale Gault." Anthony was startled.

The officer seemed pleasant enough as he smiled and walked around the table, hand outstretched. Anthony rose and accepted the officer's hand.

"Mr. Pierce, I'm sorry to intrude on you. I'm here concerning the knife incident of last night. Is Miss Claire Pierce your daughter?" Anthony nodded without speaking. "Would she be available to talk?"

"No, she isn't. She was given a strong pain medication at the hospital. It knocked her out and she's asleep."

"I'm awake, Father." Claire stood in the doorway between the hall and eating room. She slowly and with great effort walked into the room. Her arm, although wrapped and in a sling, hurt more than any pain she could remember experiencing. Her head felt twice its normal size and pulsed agonizingly.

Mrs. Wingate was the first to respond. "Pet, you shouldn't be up. And walking by yourself." As she said this, Mrs. Wingate rounded the table and went to Claire. Putting her arm round Claire's midriff, she led her to a chair. "Now you sit and I'll get you something to eat."

"Thank you." Claire looked at Lieutenant Gault. She could tell he had been watching her. Now he stood still as if thinking. Claire wondered what it was.

"Excuse me, Miss Pierce, I'm Lieutenant Dale Gault from the police department. If you don't feel up to talking just now, I can return later."

Claire sighed as Mrs. Wingate placed a cup of cocoa and buttered toast in front of her. "I suppose this is as good a time as any to go over with you what happened." She stopped talking and picked up her cup.

"Why don't we wait until you've eaten and are feeling better. Perhaps I can talk to your sister first."

Three voices in unison spoke, "No," startling the lieutenant.

"You see, Lieutenant, my sister is different. She probably doesn't even remember attacking me last night."

Gault stood with his hands on the back of a chair. "I'm not sure what to do then."

"Lieutenant, please sit down. Would you care for a cup of cocoa or coffee? I'll tell you what happened."

Gault pulled out the chair and sat. "I'll have a cup of coffee, if you please." He seemed in no hurry to leave.

Claire glanced at her father. If looks could kill, Father would be brought up on charges for the police officer's murder.

Apparently either Lieutenant Gault didn't notice or he didn't care. Taking out a pad and pencil, he took notes as Claire recounted the misadventure. She was very thorough and precise.

"How I wish all my witnesses were as detailed as you, Miss Pierce."

After finishing her narrative, Claire leaned back in her chair, picked up her now lukewarm cocoa and watched the lieutenant. Maybe because she knew he watched her.

The room remained quiet until Mr. Pierce broke the silence. "Well, Lieutenant, is there anything else?"

"Ah, no. Well, yes there is. What's going to be done so that something like this doesn't happen again?"

"I have already been working on that."

"You have, Father?"

"Yes, Dear. Mrs. Wingate and I have made a list of changes. I, of course, plan to go over it with you before any final decisions are made."

Lieutenant Gault pulled his gaze from Claire to her father, "But what are you going to do today, so that this doesn't happen, say, again tonight?" All was again quiet.

Claire spoke up, "Well, that's simple. My door locks. I'll keep it locked at night. Will that do Lieutenant?"

Gault nodded and stood. "Here is my card. Please don't hesitate to call if you need anything." He held it out for Claire and appeared disappointed when Mrs. Wingate took it instead.

Mrs. Wingate stood, "Lieutenant, I'll show you out. We can go down this hall. Once you go up the stairs, just follow the walk along the side of the house to the driveway." And like that he was gone.

Chapter 8

Two weeks later Claire sat in the lawn swing, holding Adrian. Eva sat beside her looking at the storybook "Goldilocks and the Three Bears." Johnnie sat on the lawn playing with his favorite puppy, Rex.

The afternoon was warm. It had rained most of the night which only seemed to have made the day steamier and hotter. Adrian had been awake several times during the night. Now he was blissfully sleeping. Claire struggled to remain awake. She was helped in this effort by the constant hammering and sawing coming from the house.

Claire became instantly alert when she saw Rev. Cameron Forester and Lily walking from the house. Rev. Forester was the new pastor. He had graduated from seminary in January. He was also single.

 She wasn't sure what to do. She didn't want to sit on the swing with the pastor. This left her staring at him as he stared at her. He was tall and slim with blonde hair combed straight back. His bright blue eyes appeared to sparkle like he was ready to get into mischief. Claire had heard that he had just celebrated his twenty-fourth birthday. Several of her friends said she should "set her cap" for him.

To Claire's surprise, and relief, Lily cleared her throat, "Miss Claire, Rev. Forester has asked me it I might be able to help out some at the church."

"Yes, Miss Pierce, we're planning a special celebration for Mrs. Heneretta Dorsey's eightieth birthday. I'm told that she has done so much for the church. We want to make her day very special. The church board has recommended Miss Lily to head-up the planning. Several ladies have told me that she is exceptionally talented in such things."

The back door opened and Ann came walking out, followed by Lieutenant Gault. "Hi, Mr. Gault. Would you like me to read my book to you?" Eva got off the swing and went to the lieutenant. Dale Gault had stopped by a couple of times since the stabbing incident. Eva had become fond of him.

"Why that would be very nice. May I talk to your…. ah, your aunt first? Before I leave, you may read it to me."

Claire noticed the lieutenant's hesitancy in what to call her. She also wondered what was she to the children?

Claire introduced the preacher and Gault. "Of course, Lily may help with the planning. Um, why don't the two of you go into the eating room to discuss it. Just let me know what's going on and when you'll be needed at the church."

"Thank you, Miss Pierce." He and Dale Gault shook hands, "Nice to meet you, Lieutenant." Rev. Forester and Lily strolled companionly back to the house. It dawned on Claire that the Reverend and Lily might make a good match.

"Come sit beside me." Eva patted the bench. Gault hesitated.

"Yes, please sit down, Lieutenant. Ann, please bring us something to drink."

Gault smiled at Claire. "Warm afternoon, isn't it?"

"The rain last night didn't do much to cool things off."

"The heat doesn't seem to be bothering the baby."

Adrian was sleeping blissfully in Claire's arms.

"No, not now. But he was awake several times during the night."

"That means you were up several times. I'll bet you're worn out. Your arm has healed without any difficulties?"

Eva sat watching them banter back and forth becoming very bored. She jumped off the swing. "I'm going to help Ann." Shaking her finger at Gault, she stated, "Remember Mr. Gault, I'm going to read you my story before you leave."

Gault gave Eva a wink. Turning back to Claire, he said, "Forester and Lily make a good-looking couple. Say, you really look tired. Want me to leave?"

"Oh no! Please stay. Did you notice the renovations as you came through the house?"

"I did. Mrs. Wingate is going to love the new kitchen. I didn't know you had an elevator. Does it work?"

"Not anymore. My grandfather had it put in for the guests to get up to the third floor.

He and my grandmother loved to host parties and dancing."

Ann returned with iced tea followed by Eva carrying napkins.

Gault took a hefty drink before asking, "What's happening with Trudy?"

"She and her nurse have moved to the house we affectionately call the doll house. My grandparents lived in it after my folks married. Trudy didn't fuss at all. I think she was glad to leave the noise. It only took three days to get the place in order. And Mrs. Wingate found a widow lady to cook and we've hired a young farm girl as a live-in maid.

The two rocked gently watching the children play. They would throw a stick and Rex would go after it. However, instead of bringing it back he sat down where he was and waited for the children to come to him. Both would run to him laughing all the way.

Finally, Gault turned to Claire and asked, "Tell me about Lily?"

Claire was startled. Was he interested in Lily?

"Well, she came to us after her father died. He was a methodist minister in North Webster. They'd lost her mother in the influenza epidemic. When the church hired a new minister, she had to vacate the parsonage."

"That seems rather cruel."

"The new minister's wife offered to let Lily stay as a maid. She didn't want to. The parsonage held too many memories. She applied for a position at a domestic employment agency and we hired her. That was two years ago."

As an afterthought Claire added, "Lily has been a real godsend. I'd hate to lose her."

Gault sat gazing at Claire, making the hair on the back of her neck tingle. "Have you had the hearing yet about getting custody of the children?"

Claire's face clouded and she let out a deep sigh. "Yes, we have. Father and I went to see Judge Mikkelsen Tuesday. Because I don't have a regular income and I'm dependent on Father for my livelihood, he wouldn't grant me custody. He did give custody to Father, however."

"I can see that you're upset."

"Well, yes! The children's mother asked me to take them. It's not as though I'm a pauper. I maintain the house and pay all the bills. My name is on Father's check book. I have access to all his funds. I know all the combinations to his safes and I have keys to all the deposit boxes at the banks." Claire's outburst startled Adrian and he cried. "Oh, I'm sorry, Sweetheart." She put him over her shoulder and talked to him lovingly while rubbing his back. He was soon quieted.

"I'm the one who should be apologizing. I have no right to intrude on your privacy. I should be going. Thank you for the ice tea. It hit the spot." He called to Eva, "Eva, before I go, are you going to read to me?"

Eva came running, "Oh, yes!" Lieutenant Gault drew the girl to his lap as she read the story.

The scene touched something deep within Claire. A feeling she had never experienced before.

Chapter 9

Claire was upstairs reading to Eva before her afternoon nap. Ann tapped lightly on the door. "Yes, come in."

"Miss Claire, there's a man here asking to see you. He wouldn't give his name and I don't know him."

"Eva, I'll finish reading this book to you when you wake up from your nap. Go to sleep now." Eva had almost been asleep when Ann had interrupted the story. She didn't complain just rolled onto her side and closed her eyes.

The two women slipped out into the hall and Claire gently closed the bedroom door. "You say that you don't know who this man is?"

"No, Miss. I've never seen him."

"Don't leave me, unless I ask you to."

"Yes, Miss."

In the middle of the parlor stood a slender man wearing a wrinkled suit. It was a size or two too large for him. He needed a haircut, a shave, and a bath. His hands were behind his back holding his hat, as he eyed various parts of the room.

"Good afternoon. I'm Claire Pierce. You wanted to see me?"

"Good afternoon, Miss Pierce. Allow me to introduce myself. I'm Jasper Taft, Eva and Adrian's father." Claire knew she was being prejudice, but his smile reminded her of a fox. Even his jaw protruded forward. "I realize I'm quite a surprise. I've been indisposed and just learned of my wife's untimely death."

Claire was at a loss for words. What was she to do? Was he here to take the children from her? Finally, she softly uttered, "What do you want?"

"What do I want? My children, of course."

This was beyond anything she could have imagined. Where was her help when she needed it? How she wished Father or Lieutenant Gault were here. For once she was glad her father had been given custody. That should buy some time. She looked this man in the face and told him, "I do not care to discuss this issue with you. You will have to return when my father is here. Come back this evening at eight o'clock. Ann, show this man out."

The man gave her a wicked smile, turned on his heels and left. Claire heard the front door open then close. She dropped to the sofa. Ann came into the parlor.

"Miss Claire, what are we going to do?"

This was exactly what she was asking herself. But there was no need to worry the girl. Claire smiled at Ann, "We are going to trust God and do whatever is necessary to save these children from that awful man."

As she sat thinking about the evening, she wished Dale Gault could be there. This thought surprised her. Why did she want him present? To be honest, her heart was drawn to him. Logic dictated; her heart should be pulled to Rev. Forester not a policeman. Still, she couldn't help how her heart felt.

Claire was waiting for Father that evening when he walked through the door. "What is it, Claire? Why do you look so alarmed?" Claire related what had ensued that afternoon. Father paced, "Who does this man think he is? He can't just waltz in here and take the children. Did he show you any identity? Do you have any proof the man is who he claims to be?"

"No, Father." That question gave her a glimmer of hope. But then, "What are we going to do if he is really their father? I couldn't bare losing the children."

"Neither could I. I'm calling Lieutenant Gault and my lawyer, Stan. I want both present tonight."

Lieutenant Gault arrived at the Pierce home at seven. With him was a police officer, Roy Wolfe, dressed as a butler. The lieutenant did not waste time on pleasantries and immediately shared his plan. "This is Officer Wolfe. He will act as your butler. I suggest we have this meeting in your office."

The four walked into Mr. Pierce's home office. "Well, this is it." Mr. Pierce told them. "It also serves as the library as is obvious by the plethora of books strewn about. Since Johnnie and Eva have come, they've kind of taken over this room when I'm not at home."

Ornate walnut bookshelves lined two walls. They were full of books to the point that some books were resting on top of the upright ones. Children's books lay on the floor as well as on two small tables.

Long windows encompassed a third wall. "I loved these windows as a kid. I used to walk out of them. Now the children do."

Gault scrutinized the desk sitting in front of the windows. "That is a very impressive desk. My grandfather, who was a physician, had a large desk but this one is massive."

"It's been in the family since the house was built. So has this carpet." A badly warn and faded red carpet covered the floor. "My wife, and now my daughter, have tried to get me to replace the carpet. But I have fond memories of my grandfather and me sitting on it while he read stories to me."

Gault returned to the business at hand, "I see a door. Where does it lead?"

Mr. Pierce nodded, "Yes. My bedroom is adjacent."

"Good. I'd like to talk to Johnnie."

Claire and her father spoke in unison, "Why?"

"Johnnie is old enough that he should know and remember Taft. He and I will hide in the bedroom. We'll have the light off and the door open just enough so Johnnie can see between the door and the jam. I want Johnnie to have a look at this man to see if he recognizes him.

I doubt if Taft, if that's his name, really wants the children. He probably is hoping you'll give him money."

"Give him money for the children! Never." Claire's passion got the better of her.

"I know you wouldn't, Miss Pierce." Gault turned to Mr. Pierce, "Mr. Pierce, it's important, you don't offer him any money. Let him bring up the subject. I want him to make the first suggestion. When he does, act indignant and angry. But, eventually haggle with him over the price. Finally agree. Whatever the amount, claim you'll need three or four days to collect the cash. That will give me time to inquire about him. Also, offer the man a drink. I want to get his fingerprints."

"We don't use alcohol in this house, Lieutenant."

Claire spoke up, "I'll have Mrs. Wingate ready with coffee."

"That will be fine. Let's hope he's a coffee drinker."

"I'll be sure he takes a cup." Claire was determined.

The doorbell rang. "That's probably my lawyer, Stanley Ferris. I've asked him to be present," Mr. Pierce explained.

Claire left the men to explain the situation to the lawyer while she went to tell Mrs. Wingate to prepare coffee. Then she had Ann get Johnnie and brought him to the lieutenant. Dale explained to Johnnie what he wanted him to do.

"No, I don't want to. He's a bad person. What if he sees me? He'll hurt me and my sister and the baby. I know he will!"

The lieutenant knelt in front of Johnnie, "Johnnie, all I'm asking you to do is to peek out of the crack between the door and the wall. The light in the bedroom will be off. He won't be able to see you. I'll be right with you. Let's try something."

Dale went into the bedroom and turned off the light leaving the door ajar. He looked out into the office through the crack between the door and the post. "Johnnie, can you see me?"

Johnnie shook his head, "No."

"Good, neither will this man be able to see you. Come into the bedroom." Claire took Johnnie's hand and the two walked into the room.

Dale left the bedroom and closed the door so there was only a slight opening. He walked into the middle of the office. "Johnnie, can you see me?"

In a voice Dale had to strain to hear, Johnnie answered, "Yes." Claire was standing beside Johnnie holding his hand. He squeezed her hand so hard it hurt. Claire's heart ached for the boy. She sent up a silent prayer for his safety.

Dale returned to the bedroom and told Claire she was free to leave. Then he bent to Johnnie's ear and whispered, "Be very quiet and still. Remember, the man won't be able to see you. We just need to know if you recognize him."

All was set. The man arrived promptly at eight o'clock. The costumed policeman butler showed the alleged Mr. Taft into the office. Claire introduced him to her father and the family lawyer.

She had to keep from glancing at the bedroom door. Dale stood behind Johnnie in the bedroom with his hands on Johnnie's shoulders hoping to reassure him.

The butler left and momentarily returned with a tray of coffee that he sat on a small table. Claire served the coffee.

"None for me, thanks." Claire shoved a cup towards Taft as though she hadn't heard.

He peered at her pushing the cup away. "Are you daft girl? I said I didn't want any."

Her heart sank. She had failed. Did any of his prints get onto the cup when he had shoved it away. The butler took the tray and Claire sat miserable at failing in her one assignment.

Mr. Ferris spoke, "I've been informed you claim to be Eva's and Adrian's father. What proof do you have." Mr. Taft got out his wallet and produced his driver's license. "Licenses can be faked," Mr. Ferris remarked.

"Well, it's not faked!"

"Didn't you abandon Nadine, their mother, when she told you she was expecting Adrian?"

"So, what if I did? They're my kids and I want them now."

"What means do you have to care for these children?" Mr. Ferris emphasized children.

"Well, what's that to you? Maybe I can't give them all the stuff Pierce can. But I want them."

"Mr. Pierce is prepared to go to court to maintain custody of Eva and Adrian. He has the means to spend as much money as necessary. Do you?"

Jasper Taft was silent for a long time. Finally, he scowled at Father and spoke, "I can see how they might be better off here. It's true I don't have much money to fight you in court. How much would it be worth to you, if I just disappeared?"

Father stared at Taft from behind his desk. His thoughts concerning the children's money-grabbing so called parent was readable on his face. He stood and spoke,

"Mr. Taft, I find what you are suggesting repulsive. How long do you think a man would get in prison for selling his children?"

Taft stood and leaned over towards Mr. Pierce, his hands palms down on the top of the desk. Claire gasped. Finger prints! Claire was thankful there was a desk between the man and her father.

"Mister, you're a rich man. You have no idea what it's like not knowing where your next meal is coming from. Sure, I'll sell these kids. If you want them, you'll pay me $5,000 by tomorrow. And if you go to the police, you'll be sorry!"

"That's outrageous. I can't get $5,000 by tomorrow. You'll have to give me at least three days to raise that much."

Mr. Ferris piped up, right on cue, "Now just a minute, Anthony. What he's suggesting is illegal."

"Ferris, I think you might be more comfortable stepping out of the room." Anthony glared at his friend until the lawyer got up and walked out into the hall. Claire, I think you should leave also." Claire got up and walked out into the hall, miffed.

Mr. Ferris heard voices in the parlor. He thought one of them was Preston. The butler and Preston were standing quietly talking. "Well, hello, Preston. I thought you'd be back in college by now."

"I was going to leave this afternoon until I heard about that man. What's going on in there? Why did you come out?"

"Taft has implied he won't exercise his parental rights if your father pays him money."

The butler suggested, "We'd better step away from the door. When Taft comes out, it wouldn't be wise for him to see us. He might get spooked."

No sooner had the four stepped out of sight when the office door opened. Taft walked out and frowned back into the room. "I'll be here Thursday. You better have my money ready or I won't wait for any court. I'll take the kids and you'll never see them again!" Taft turned on his heel and hurriedly exited out the front door. The top part of the door was frosted glass with a fleur-de-lis etched in it. As Taft slammed it shut, a crack appeared diagonally from the top left to the bottom right.

Johnnie and Lieutenant Gault had joined Father when Claire, Ferris, Preston, and Officer Wolfe entered the room. Father came around the side of the desk and knelt on one knee in front of Johnnie. "Do you know that man? Is he Eva's daddy?"

Wide eyed with fear, Johnnie replied, "No. His name is Buck Smith. He's a friend of Uncle Jasper. He came over to the house a lot, sometimes even when Uncle Jasper wasn't there. He and Uncle Jasper yelled at each other a lot and even got into fights. When he would leave, Uncle Jasper would yell at Momma and hit her and pull her hair. I used to hide Eva and me so he wouldn't hit us. I think Momma liked Buck but I don't. You aren't going to let Eva and Adrian go with him are you, Mr. Pierce?"

"Don't you worry, Johnnie. No one is going to take any of you from us. This is your home now. And I really would like you to call me Grandpa, if you would be comfortable doing that."

Johnnie's eyes lit up, "I've never had a grandpa. One of my friends has three grandpas. Can Eva call you Grandpa, too?"

"Well, of course she can."

"I'll go upstairs and tell her."

Claire spoke up, "I think you'd better wait until morning. Eva is sleeping."

After seeing Johnnie to bed, Claire sat in her darkened bedroom. She was upset at what her father had told Johnnie. She couldn't really understand why. It was good for Johnnie and the other two children to have a grandfather. But what was she? Claire had no desire to be called "Aunt Claire." In her heart she knew she wanted to be "Momma."

Chapter 10

"I don't want to go to school! I want to stay here. Can't Preston keep teaching me?" It was Johnnie's first day of school.

"Johnnie, we've been over this before. Preston will be leaving for college in a couple of days. He'll be disappointed after taking you to the barber to get this nice hair-cut. Besides, you'll be making a lot of new friends."

"But I'm older than all the other kids in my class. You said I should be in the fourth or fifth grade and I'm only in the second."

"Preston has done a good job helping you to read and do your numbers. Make him proud of you. No one has to know your age." Johnnie was small for his age. Claire wasn't too concerned about him being bigger than the other children in his class.

"Who's going to school today?" Mrs. Wingate came into the eating room carrying a popular children's lunch box. It was a red tin box with football players painted on it. "Johnnie, I've made your favorite sandwich, beef with mustard, for your lunch. And there is also two sugar cookies and an apple." Johnnie still fretted.

Eva cried, "I don't want Johnnie to leave. I'm afraid he won't ever come back."

Claire thought, this is harder than I thought it would be. "Eva, you and I can walk

Johnnie to school. This afternoon we'll return to get him when school is out."

Mrs. Wingate surprised Eva with a pink box she had made up containing the same lunch as Johnnie.

After returning from seeing Johnnie to school, Claire knew she needed something to keep her busy and her mind off last night's events. She found Lily and Ann. "I've decided to move my bedroom down to Mother's suite. The dressing room is large enough to be used as a nursery," Claire announced.

The three entered the renovated suite. "Oh, Miss Claire, I've never been in here. This room is beautiful," uttered Ann in awe. The original wallpaper had been reglued. New, dove gray Axminster carpet was laid. White lace curtains hung at the windows.

Mother's lavish handmade furniture had been cleaned and polished.

"I want to help," voiced the ever-present Eva.

"You sure can. We don't have to bring my bedroom furniture down, just Adrian's things. Ann, you and Eva take care of that."

The team spent the morning traipsing up and down the stairs moving Claire's personal belongings and Adrian's baby things. After the third trip, Claire emphatically declared, "I'm going to get the old elevator repaired."

Just after ten the front door banged open. Johnnie came hurdling in and up the stairs to the bathroom. When he came out, Claire stood in the hall waiting for him, "What are you doing home?"

"I had to go to the bathroom."

"Johnnie! There are bathrooms at school. At certain times during the day your teacher will take the whole class to the restrooms. There are different rooms for the boys and the girls. Didn't she tell you?"

"She did. But I couldn't wait."

"All you needed to do was to raise your hand and ask her to use the restroom."

"I'm wasn't going to do that in front of all those girls!"

Claire drove Johnnie back to school. She explained the misunderstanding to the office secretary. Claire asked what had happened not be made public. She was concerned Johnnie would be humiliated in front of the class.

After school Johnnie came bounding out of the front door amongst several other children. Running up to Claire and Eva, Johnnie shouted, "Guess what! I have a new name. From now on I'm not Johnnie anymore. I'm Jack!"

Eva put her hands on her hips, leaned forward and with a scowl asked, "What do you mean you have a new name?"

Johnnie laughed, "There are three Johns in my room. Teacher said we all can't be called John because we wouldn't know which one she was talking to. So, she put three names in a hat and me and the other Johns took turns pulling a name out. I got to go first because I'm the oldest. I picked out the name Jack. Teacher said it's a nick-name for John. So, from now on call me Jack!"

"Do you like that name? You don't have to accept the name if you don't want to." Claire was concerned about his emotional condition. He had been confronted with so many changes and was just now seeming to be getting some stability.

"I sure do like it! It's a grown-up name. Better then Johnnie, that's for little kids. That's the name John Johnson picked. He didn't like it and said he wanted a different name. Teacher asked him what his middle name was. It's Edward. Teacher said he could be called Edward. Ed thought that was pretty good. During play time he told us boys to call him Ed. He said his dad is Edward but everyone calls him Ed."

"Who is the third John in your class?"

"John Reynolds. He's the only one that's going to be called John."

"I want a new name, too," voiced Eva.

"Well, you're not old enough yet. Now remember call me JACK! There is so much more I want to tell you. School is fun and the kids in my class are real nice."

The two children and Claire turned into the driveway and saw a taxi sitting near the front door. "Now why is a cab at our door?" She was quite sure it wouldn't be Jasper Taft. At least she hoped not. "Johnnie, I mean Jack, take Eva around the sidewalk to the back door. Stay with Mrs. Wingate until I come to get you. Hurry, children."

Claire entered the vestibule. Sitting on a chair and surrounded by boxes of various sizes was Aunt Charlotte. Beside her stood a perturbed cab driver and a vary baffled Ann, holding an unhappy Adrian.

He let everyone within ear shot know about his unhappiness. "Ann, the children are downstairs having a snack. Please go down there. Maybe seeing them will quiet Adrian. Thank you.

"Aunt Charlotte, what a nice surprise." This was said with questioning sincerity. "What brings you here now? We didn't expect you until Thanksgiving. Why didn't you send a telegram to let us know you were coming?"

It was customary for Father's widowed sister, Charlotte, to visit near Thanksgiving and stay until just after the New Year. She then normally left to live in Florida during the winter months.

"Claire, please pay the taxi driver. I don't have any cash on me."

Rummaging through her purse, Claire thought to herself, no money! Father said that Uncle Carl left her well provided for. She also collected a big inheritance when grandfather died. Claire knew better than to say anything out loud.

After receiving his fare and a generous tip, the cab driver gave both a polite tip of his hat and left. The two women stared at each other.

"Come into the living room, Auntie, and tell me what's wrong."

They sat facing each other. Claire waiting. Finally, Charlotte slumped her shoulders, "I've been living in a hotel."

"A hotel! That's terrible! Why?"

In a more resolute voice Charlotte continued, "I suppose you'll find out sooner or later. I'm surprised you don't already know. I'm broke, bankrupt!"

Claire's eyes opened wide in astonishment. "Bankrupt. How can that be?"

Charlotte laughed, "To be honest, I've misspent all my income on pretty clothes, costly jewelry, stray animals, and dubious other pursuits. I've lived thinking only of myself. You know, I've always felt awkward in society. It seems I couldn't hold a cup without spilling the contents. You might say to overcome my feelings of a lack of confidence, I developed a guise of arrogance and self-importance."

Claire felt sorry for her aunt. What she had just confessed was so true. She had always worn gaudy clothes, although expensive. And her taste in jewelry, also expensive, was flashy and garish.

Charlotte began to cry, "At seventy-seven, I'm destitute and have no place to go. I haven't had anything to eat since yesterday, and I'm so hungry."

Claire came round the coffee table and hugged Charlotte, "Auntie, that's terrible. Let's go downstairs to the eating room."

"You still eat in the basement!" Claire did not respond to this remark, only leading the way to the stairs.

"Haven't you gotten that elevator working yet? I'm getting too old to go up and down stairs. What is all that pounding? Whose baby is that and what children are in the basement?"

"We've had some changes. The letter Father sent must not have reached you. He wasn't sure where you were. I'll explain everything as you eat."

In a much softer voice, Aunt Charlotte answered, "Well, I've been living in several different hotels."

Claire explained about the children as she and Mrs. Wingate, watched in amazement as Aunt Charlotte woofed down a bowl of soup, a ham sandwich and four cookies. When she finally came up for breath, Charlotte smiled at Mrs. Wingate, "That was very good, Mrs. Wingate. Thank you for taking the time to prepare it for me."

Claire eyed Aunt Charlotte in bewilderment, as Mrs. Wingate stared stupefied. Never could they remember Aunt Charlotte acting any way but entitled. This was something new. Claire played back the last hour. Aunt Charlotte had no money for the cab fare. She hadn't eaten all day. And she was living in a hotel.

"Claire, I'm very tired. Could I rest? When Anthony gets home, I'll explain everything that's happened to me. I'm just not up to climbing those stairs just now. Is there some place down here where I can retire?"

This last comment floored Claire. Mrs. Wingate spoke up, "Mrs. Ainsworth, come this way. You're welcome to rest in my room." Claire sat staring at nothing. Then she remembered the elevator. She hurried up the stairs. Maybe, if there wasn't much wrong with the elevator, the repair company could get it working yet today.

Aunt Charlotte was still sleeping when her brother arrived home just after six that evening. Claire followed him into the library. She started to tell her father the events of the day. He held up his hand to stop her, "I already know about Charlotte.

175

Her banker called me yesterday. I know she's bankrupt. Her house has been sold as have all the contents. She has also had to sell much of her jewelry to pay off debts. I feared this was going to happen and expected that sooner or later she would be showing up here."

"What are you going to do?"

"What can I do? I can't very well put her out in the cold. I'll have a serious talk with her first. I want you to be present. There'll be no misunderstanding about her status here. Where should we put her?"

"I've already put her boxes in Trudy's and Olivia's old apartment."

"I thought you were going to let Cecilia have those rooms? She thanked me just yesterday for the area. She's really looking forward to having her girlfriends over."

"Well, I had to make the decision quickly. I suppose I could tell Cecilia to move her things in Trudy's apartment. Then put Aunt Charlotte in Cecilia's room. Aunt Charlotte will be miffed about that."

"Let her! He glanced at the door and Claire followed his line of sight. "Why, look who's here. Good evening, Charlotte. I hear you've fallen on some hard times."

Charlotte entered still looking tired. She straightened and squared her shoulders at her brother's comment. "Good evening, Anthony. How do you know? Has Claire tattled all my problems to you?"

"Your banker called me."

"Oh."

"Come in. Let's sit down over there." He pointed to a corner of the room occupied by two upholstered chairs and a small couch. Before sitting down Anthony closed the pocket doors. The siblings each chose a chair. Claire sat on the couch. "We need to have a heart-to-heart talk."

"Father, should I ring for coffee?"

Charlotte looked at her brother, rather pathetically, "I wouldn't mind some coffee and maybe a little something to eat."

Father studied his sister closely. Claire had noted sagging jowls and several new wrinkles since she had seen her last Christmas. She was sure Father had noticed the same. Her once auburn hair was laced with gray. A worn dress hung on her. She had obviously lost weight. Claire couldn't help but grieve for her. This former beauty was her aunt and she loved her.

After a sigh, Father nodded for her to ring for coffee and a snack.

He cleared his throat and took his sister's hand, "Charlotte, you have always gotten whatever you needed. No, what you've always wanted. Ainsworth provided for you more than adequately in his will. You inherited more money from father and Mother. You had more than enough to live a comfortable life. Instead, you've squandered it all!"

Aunt Charlotte burst out crying. She put her hands over her face, "I know, I know." Peeking up at her brother, she miserably murmured, "Help me, please."

There was a knock at the door. To prevent anyone from seeing her aunt cry, Claire quickly went to the door, "Thank you, Ann. I'll take the tray." Then she busied herself pouring coffee before removing a linen cloth from a tray of gingersnap cookies.

Father pulled his sister's attention back to him, "Charlotte, I won't put you out or let you go hungry. You may stay here with us. Cecilia is moving into Trudy's rooms. You may have her room."

Charlotte's old self surfaced, "That's only one room! Why can't I have Trudy's rooms or your dead wife's apartment? Besides, I can't climb up and down those stairs all day." Anthony merely maintained eye contact.

Charlotte must have realized how she was behaving. She lowered her head and whispered, "I'm sorry. Cecilia's room will suit me fine."

"Aunt Charlotte, men are here now, working on the elevator. They don't think it will take much to get it operating properly." Her aunt bobbed her thanks.

Father was not finished though. "Charlotte, do you have any jewelry or furs left?"

"I have one fur, a couple of rings, this bracelet, and the three necklaces of Mother's. Why?"

"Because I want them. I will get them appraised and sell them."

"NO!"

Father put a hand on each of his knees, leaned forward glaring at his sister, "Bring the necklaces here for me to see. We will choose one for you to keep. The other things will be sold. Whatever we realize from them, I'll set a monthly allowance for you. This you can use for your personal needs. But mind you, if you spend all your allowance the first week, you will NOT get anymore until the next month. Do you understand?"

Charlotte looked at her brother defiantly before her expression changed, "Yes, Anthony, I understand. Thank you. I do appreciate you helping me."

Chapter 11

Father mentioned that Dale Gault would be coming by that evening with information regarding the children's father. He arrived at 7:30. Claire's normal demeanor left at 7:31. Never had she experienced such longings. Claire and Dale stood looking at each other. Was he having any of these same feelings for her? She didn't even know if he was married. She hadn't seen a ring on his finger but many men did not wear wedding bands.

Father cleared his throat, "Let's go into the office. Ann will be bringing us a tray of coffee."

Just then the elevator door opened and Aunt Charlotte wandered into the hall. Speaking with a mild smirk, she asked, "Who is this? Claire, are you finally being courted?"

Claire froze sure she would burst into flames at any moment.

"Charlotte! Don't be rude. Claire and I have business to discuss with this gentleman. I'm sure, if you try, you can find something useful to occupy your time." Father turned his back to his sister and ushered Claire and the young lieutenant into his office and to the corner sitting area. "Please, excuse my sister. She can be very uncouth. Heaven knows my mother tried to teach her differently. Please sit down." Just then a polite knock was heard. "That will be Ann with the coffee."

Claire hopped up before her father could answer. It was something to do and got her out of proximity to Lieutenant Gault. Despite her shaking hands, she served the coffee. Both daughter and parent looked concerningly at the lieutenant.

Dale smiled warmly at Claire easing her nerves the tiniest bit, then looked at Father. "The news is good." Father leaned back in his chair visibly relaxing. "As Jack told us, the man's name is Boris "Buck" Smith. He was in the Newbury County jail with the children's father, Jasper Taft.

While there Taft read of his wife's death and about the children coming to live with you folks. He bragged to the other inmates and some guards about coming here and threatening to take the children."

He paused to put sugar in his coffee, took a sip and continued, "When he and Smith were being transferred from the jail to the court house for trial, they managed to overpower a guard. Smith made good his escape. Taft was shot and killed." Lieutenant Gault stopped and studied first Father then Claire. Waiting for their reaction.

However, all Claire could think of were Eva and little Adrian. "Those poor, poor children. Both parents failed them. How very sad."

Father took Claire's hand and smiled tenderly at her, "Yes, Sweetheart. But we won't fail them." Still holding his daughter's hand, he turned to Gault, "What is the plan for tomorrow?"

"Smith will be here at 7:30. Officer Wolfe will again dress as your butler. I'll be in the bedroom, as before. There will be two officers hiding outside. Miss Pierce, you don't need to be present."

"Why? I want to."

"No, if there's trouble, it will be safer if as few people as necessary are present."

Claire sighed. Of course, he was right but she didn't have to like it.

Alarmed, fear gleamed in Father's eyes. "Do you really think the man might try something?"

"Mr. Pierce if nothing else, when he is found out, I'm sure he will try to run. He may even have a gun."

"I never thought of that." Father turned to Claire. "Where do you think the safest place would be?"

"I think everyone should leave the house and go to the doll house. I'll plan something. Possibly a surprise welcome party for Aunt Charlotte. She'll love the attention and it will give her and the children an opportunity to get acquainted."

If only Trudy will be able to handle that.

Chapter 12

"I feel we're as ready for Smith as we can be." Gault surveyed the office. "Preston, I still wish you would leave."

"Lieutenant, I'm not going to hide. I'll stay in the parlor. I'm the biggest and probably in the best physical condition of all the men."

"You're probably right. I just hope there'll not be any need for your aid. If Smith comes with a gun, I sure don't want you or your father getting hurt." Silently, Gault sent up a prayer. He couldn't remember the last time having done such a thing. This family was really getting under his skin.

"Just one more thing." Gault placed a chair some distance from Anthony Pierce's desk. "Mr. Pierce that evening offer this chair to Smith. Then you sit down on the other side of your desk"

Smith strolled self-importantly into the Pierce foyer. He ignored Officer Wolfe, dressed again as the butler, and sauntered toward Mr. Pierce, who was standing at the office entrance.

Smith had shaved, gotten a haircut and cleaned his suit. He had forgotten about his shoes. They were grimy with mud. Wolfe noted the bulge of a gun under Smith's suit coat. He gave Mr. Pierce a discreet nod as he inconspicuously touched his side. Mr. Pierce responded with affirmation.

Before Pierce had even sat down, Buck demanded, "Well, you got the money or do I take my kids? You'd better believe me. I'm not messing around. I'll take them and you'll never see them again."

Anthony Pierce called Buck by his presumed name, "Mr. Taft, I believe you. However, before I give you the money, what assurance do I have that you will leave and never come here again?"

Buck Smith looked at Anthony with a sneer, "Ya don't! Other than my word. Besides I'm shucking this place. I'm bound for better places than this dump of a town. Now out with the money. I've got a train to catch."

Mr. Pierce picked up a large white envelope sitting on his desk, "The money is in this envelope." Buck jumped up and grabbed the envelope, gave a slight salute with his right hand, and turned toward the door.

Officer Wolfe stepped into the room, blocking the exit. Lieutenant Gault entered the office from his hiding place in the bedroom. Both men held guns in their hands. "Hands up, Buck."

Gault watched as Buck pitched his hat at Officer Wolfe, momentarily knocking him off balance. Instinctively Wolfe raised his arm to push the hat away. This gave Buck the chance he needed. Gault was startled at Buck's quickness and agility. In two steps Buck was at the door. "Watch out, he has a gun!" Wolfe shouted as he was grabbed by Buck and pushed against the wall.

Gault also had a gun but was unable to shoot fearing he would hit Officer Wolfe. "Mr. Pierce, get down!"

Still moving, Buck turned and shot twice. Gault felt a bullet whiz by slamming into a first edition book behind him. To his horror, he saw a second bullet hit Mr. Pierce in the head. The bullet continued, shattering the middle window sending broken pieces of glass on to the desk, the chair, the carpet, and Mr. Pierce who had collapsed. Smith sprinted to the front door, which still held the cracked window.

Gault, trusting the other officers would be able to stop the fleeing man, dashed to help Mr. Pierce. Fortunately, the bullet had only grazed the side of his head. However, he was bleeding profusely, partly due to the numerous cuts from the broken glass.

While Gault ministered to Mr. Pierce, he could see the action unfolding in the hall. Preston made a flying tackle grabbing Buck around his waist as he tried to get out the front door. The two of them were rolling around the marble floor. They slammed into a table in the center of the room tipping over a vase of flowers. Water and flowers came cascading on to the pair.

The two policemen who had been stationed outside came running in. In a matter of seconds, Buck was restrained and unceremoniously dragged to his feet. He and Preston were dripping with water and bits of flower petals. The white envelope had torn and paper lay scattered about. Buck was hand cuffed and unwillingly escorted out.

"Wolfe, call over to that other house and have Miss. Pierce and their nurse get over here." Gault turned his attention back to Mr. Pierce. Using his handkerchief, he tried unsuccessfully to stem the flow of blood. Several pieces of glass had imbedded themselves in his flesh making it difficult to apply pressure.

When the two women arrived, they found Gault and Preston picking out tiny flecks of glass from Father's face, neck, and hands

Once Olivia had the bleeding stopped and the wounds attended to, she declared, "The glass cuts are worse than the bullet injury. Mr. Pierce you need to go to the hospital."

With an air of self-satisfaction, he refused. "I'll visit Dr. Fletcher tomorrow."

"I must apologize. I'm so embarrassed, Mr. Pierce. That shot could have killed you," Gault voiced.

Preston was the real hero. Lieutenant Gault watched enviously as Claire lavished Preston with a kiss and hugs. He wondered if she would have been as free with her kisses if he had been the hero.

The next morning, Preston sat at the breakfast table with the day's paper scattered across it. Claire came in. "Preston! What are you doing with these papers strewn about like this? Father will be very upset. You know he likes to be the first person to read them."

"So, I'll iron them! I want to see if there's anything about last night. I want to take it to school and show the guys what a hero I am." Disappointed, he tossed the papers aside. "There's not one word."

"You're the hero just the same." Mrs. Wingate had come into the room. "Just to show you how much we appreciate you, I'm fixing your favorite meal, fried pork chops, mashed potatoes with pork gravy and apple pie with ice cream for supper."

Father and Claire were thankful for the lack of coverage.

The next morning, Preston reluctantly packed his car and left for college. Jack and Eva stood on the porch waving until they could no longer see the car. Eva was crying. Jack put a reassuring arm around her shoulder. "It will be okay, Sister. It will be okay."

Chapter 13

It was Claire's practice to write Preston each Sunday afternoon relating the news from home.

Dear Preston,

How is football practice going? Father and I hope to attend at least one game. I'm sure Jack and Eva will insist on coming.

Jack is thriving at school. If anyone calls him Johnnie, he pretends not to hear them until they catch on and say Jack. It's taken Eva and Father several days to

*make the change. You will be so proud
of him; his personality has bloomed.
Being older than the other students in
his class he's become a leader.*

*At first, he was sometimes mischievous.
Does that remind you of anyone? He
told me the teacher took him aside
and said, "Jack you are a leader, so be
a good one." Since then, most of the
time he's tried to do the right thing. He
craves praise.*

*Eva is enjoying Sunday School. She even
has a special friend. She isn't so clingy
with Jack.*

*Adrian can sit up by himself and roll
from side to side. Dr. Fletcher has
suggested we start him on solid food
beginning with puréed rice mixed
with milk.*

Aunt Charlotte is being very annoying. Ann and Lily frequently come upon her searching through cupboards and closets in all parts of the house. One day Ann saw her stepping out of the elevator covered in dust and cobwebs. When she asked if she needed help, Auntie ignored her as if she hadn't heard. They've asked me to speak to her. I intend to tomorrow.

We all miss you. Study hard!

Your loving sister,
Claire

Monday morning Jack came running into the breakfast room. "Miss Claire! Aunt Charlotte is in Grandpa's office pulling out books and tossing them on the floor."

Claire sighed and hurried to the library. "Aunt Charlotte, what are you doing? This place is a mess."

"Let the maids clean it up. Isn't that why you have servants?"

"Actually, no it isn't. We have been taught to clean up our own messes."

Charlotte stood on a step stool with a book in each hand. She carefully put the books back and stepped off the stool. "Oh, I'm sorry, I guess my old ways are flaring up."

Together the women picked up the books and began reshelving them. Jack and Eva had followed Claire and were also helping.

"Let's go have breakfast and you can tell me what this frantic search mission of yours is all about."

While the children ate and the ladies drank coffee, Charlotte began. "I'm looking for something."

"That's obvious. Lily said you messed up the linen closet just after she had folded all the linen. Those, incidentally, had just been ironed."

Eva popped up, "I heard Ann and Lily complaining you've been in their rooms going through their belongings."

Claire was thunderstruck, "You can't do that!"

"Why not? They're employees."

"They are not your employees. Even if they were, you just can't do that."

Charlotte hung her head and failed to respond.

"Perhaps if you'll tell me, Ann, Lilly and I can help you find whatever it is you're looking for."

"I'll help, too." Eva was ignored.

Aunt Charlotte picked up a slice of toast and took a bite without saying anything. She licked her lips, took a drink of coffee, and finally asked, "Have you ever heard about silver bells that have been passed down from generation to generation on the female side of our family?"

Claire scrunched her face as if in thought and answered, "No, I don't ever remember being told anything about bells."

Aunt Charlotte put down her cup, sighed and sat back, "There is a story that many years ago someone on the female side of our family brought eight bells to America from England. When this ancestor's daughter married, she gave the bells to her as a wedding gift. From then on as the oldest daughter wed, she was given the bells. When I married Mr. Ainsworth, my mother, your grandmother, should have given the bells to me. She told me that I was not worthy of them and she wouldn't let me have them. They must be some place in this house because I can remember playing with them as a child at Christmas." Claire looked skeptically at her aunt. "Ask your father, he'll remember playing with them," Charlotte added.

Claire couldn't understand what was so important about some old bells. She assumed Aunt Charlotte may just be getting senile and decided to humor her. "When father gets home this evening, we can ask him if he knows anything about the bells. We might even make a game out of searching for them and the children can help us."

Anthony scarcely got through the door before Charlotte pounced on him. "Yes, I do remember playing with some bells as a boy. I can't remember the last time I saw them. Maybe Ma took then with her when she moved to the doll house."

Aunt Charlotte was in a frenzy. "Let's go now! I know just were to look."

Anthony firmly said, "No! Claire can go over to have a word with Olivia. If she agrees then and only then may you go. And, let me add, you will tidy up any mess you make. I'll not have the maid over there quit because of you."

The three adults heard screaming coming from the upstairs. They rushed out of the parlor into the hall. A tearful Ann came hurrying down carrying a crying Adrian. She was followed by Lily, who was ringing her hands.

An hysterical Eva trailed next holding a rag doll and crying fiercely, "Adrian is going to die."

Adrian reached out his arms for Claire. She held him close, "There, there, sweetheart. Whatever it is, it's going to be alright."

Mr. Pierce picked up Eva and not nearly as soothingly said, "Stop that balling! It doesn't sound like Adrian is anywhere near death."

Claire turned to Ann, "For goodness sakes, what's wrong? Why is Eva saying Adrian is going to die?"

"Oh, gracious me, Adrain bit off one of the doll's button eyes and swallowed it! Lily said he'll have to have another surgery to get it out. Oh, Miss Claire I'm so sorry. I should have been watching him better. Shouldn't we take him to the hospital?"

Claire held Adrian out at arm's length and laughed, "You little rascal!" She again held him close and smiled at Ann, then Lily, "No, he doesn't have to go to the hospital. The button will just pass through him. For the next several days we'll check his diaper to watch for it."

A frowning Eva asked, "What about my doll? She only has one eye."

Claire turned to her, "When Lily has time, you ask her to let you go through the button box and look for a button that matches the doll's eye. If you can't find one you like, you could sew two new buttons on her."

"This button is blue. I think I would like her to have brown eyes like Mr. Policeman Gault. He's so pretty and so nice. I like him."

Claire stared at Eva. "He does have pretty brown eyes and is very nice." To herself she thought, yes, he is wonderful. The longing in her body returned.

Chapter 14

Claire stood in the center of the refurbished ball room. "Isn't this beautiful, Lily. It glows. Look how beautiful the floor is. Can't you just imagine people waltzing around with the band playing?"

"Yes, Miss. I especially like the painted scene on the wall. It is so pleasant to look at. Wouldn't it be lovely to have a wedding up here?"

"Strange you should say that. My mother told me this is where her and Father's wedding reception was. She said it was very hot and everyone was drinking a lot. The result was a line outside the gentlemen's facility." Both women laughed.

Lily stood with a perplexed look on her face. "Why wasn't there a ladies' line?"

"I asked my mom about that. She said that it took women so much effort to undo all their under garments that they didn't drink as much. A maid had to be available to help them undo then redo their garments." Both women laughed, again.

"I can't understand why Father refused to allow the lavatories to be redone. They really are a mess. No wedding could be held up here and expect people to use them. I'd be embarrassed. I also wish we could have saved the chandeliers. But the expense didn't justify it. Do you like the new lighting?"

"Yes. You know you say God always has a plan, even if we don't see it. Maybe leaving the bathrooms undone is for a reason."

"You may be right.

The family ate their first supper in the newly decorated dining room.

"I'm certainly glad the reconstruction on this house is finally finished. I've grown so tired of listening to hammering all day."

"Aunt Charlotte, I am, too. Diane has had such a hard time going to sleep for her nap." Everyone looked at Eva.

"And who, may I ask is Diane?" Aunt Charlotte replied in a condescending manner.

"My dolly! How do you like the wall paper I picked out?"

"If it had been up to me, I would not have allowed a three-year-old to choose what paper was used."

Giving his sister a stern look. Father admonished her, "Charlotte, that is unkind."

"Well, at least you didn't discard the mahogany dining room furniture. Great-great Grandma Pierce would roll over in her grave if you'd chucked that. It is from Italy, you know."

Ignoring his sister, Anthony turned to his daughter, "I'm pleased you decided to keep the furniture in the living room. I remember how happy your mother was when we bought it. The fabric you selected for the reupholstering is beautiful."

"Thank you, Father."

Jack spoke up, "Aunt Charlotte, Ann's and Lily's rooms have also been redecorated.

Miss Claire took them to Marques Furniture Store and let them pick out new bedroom sets. Can you believe it!"

"Excuse me." Charlotte pushed her chair back and walked to the door with her head up and back straight. Before exiting she turned and said, "When I was young, children were to be seen and not heard."

The family forgot about Aunt Charlotte and went on with the meal.

"Why don't Ann and the others eat with us?" Questioned Jack. "Don't they like us anymore?"

"It's not that," stated Claire. "The employes have elected to eat their meals in the new kitchen. I assured them they were welcome to continue to eat with us. It's easier for then and I think they are more comfortable there."

"The staff not eating with us pleases Aunt Charlotte beyond no end!"

"Cecilia that will do."

'Yes, Father."

Chapter 15

The household calm was again upset in early November.

"Claire, that was a terrible meal tonight. The soup was over salted, the potatoes were lumpy and the roast tough. Is Mrs. Wingate sick or something?"

"Aunt Charlotte, you don't have to tell me. I know something is wrong. I plan to talk to her, as soon as I get the children settled." Claire thought it was fortunate Father was out for the evening. One of the many times he had been absent in the past several weeks.

Claire knocked softly. Mrs. Wingate opened her apartment door, "Come in, Pet. I figured you'd be coming. I made some tea for us. I'm sorry about tonight's supper. I know it was terrible. Please sit down."

"What's wrong, Mrs. Wingate? Are you not feeling well?"

"My health is fine. It's my daughter and her husband. I got a letter from them today. They're losing their positions."

Mrs. Wingate's daughter, Maude was a housekeeper in the home of Conrad Spurlock, a sea merchant in Boston. Maude's husband, Jarvis Heath was the butler. Jarvis had served in the Great War with his employer. He had saved Spurlock's life during an intensive stormy sea battle. His heroism cost him his right arm. In gratitude for saving his life, Spurlock offered him a position as his butler. Jarvis knew nothing about the duties of a butler. Spurlock gave him a book, *Mrs. Beeton's Book of Household Management*. Jarvis read it from cover to cover and began his new duties. There he met and married the housekeeper, Maude. They now had a five-year-old daughter, Wanda.

"What happened? Are they being fired? You always said your son-in-law's employer was so indebted for saving his life."

"They're not being fired, exactly. Mr. Spurlock has been offered a very distinguished position in London. Maude wrote that he will earn twice what he does here. And the job comes with a house and servants. Mr. Spurlock is giving them both generous severances pay, and fine references. What are they to do? Who will hire a one-armed butler? Where will they ever be able to find a position together?"

Mrs. Wingate put her handkerchief to her face and wept.

It broke Claire's heart to see Mrs. Wingate so distressed, "Don't cry, Mrs. Wingate. It will be alright." She sat in silence thinking. Without considering what she was about to do she said, "Maude and Jarvis could come here. We could use a butler and a housekeeper. Heaven knows Father could use help from a valet. And Wanda would be a good companion for Eva."

"Do you really think Mr. Pierce would agree to that?"

"I'll talk to him when he gets home tonight."

Claire waited for her father to arrive. It was after ten o'clock when she heard the car drive up. Several nights each week Father had been going out. Claire wondered about this. But, right now she had to address Maude's and Jarvis's problem. Before her father had time to insert his key in the lock, she opened the door. "Claire! Why are you up? Is something wrong?"

"No, Father. Everything is fine. However, there is something urgent we need to discuss. Come in to the parlor." Anthony placed his coat and hat on a hall chair and followed Claire into the room. Claire had a warm fire going in the fireplace. They sat across from each other. Claire smiled. She now had second thoughts about what she wanted to say. Maybe it would have been better to have waited until breakfast. Well, it was too late now. She had committed herself, so she plunged ahead. "Did you have an enjoyable evening? You're quite dressed up?"

"Yes, it was very pleasant. Now get on with whatever is so urgent it must be discussed right now."

"Mrs. Wingate received a letter today from her daughter, Maude. You remember her, don't you."

"Yes, she married that sailor who lost his arm in the war."

Claire related the information from the letter and the need to find new employment. Father looked at his daughter suspiciously, "What exactly does that have to do with us?"

"Do you remember a sermon Pastor Forester preached about a month ago on Esther?"

"I faintly remember, why?"

"Remember, she was a Jewess but no one knew it. She married the king who was not Jewish. Then there was some trouble and one of the king's advisors convinced the king to massacre all the Jews."

"What is your point? I'm tired and want to go to bed."

"Well, Esther's Uncle Mordecai came to see her. He said she needed to go to the king and plead for her people. She was afraid that the king might kill her. Mordecai told her that maybe she had come to her royal position for such a time as this."

"What are you trying to tell me?"

"We need to hire Maude and her husband." Before Father could protest, Claire hurried on. "Besides being our butler, Jarvis could also act as your valet. You know some days you leave the house not looking your best. He could see that all your clothes are pressed and ready for you."

Claire leaned across the coffee table that separated them and continued, "Father, I really need help, now that there are three children living with us. It would be so good to have a housekeeper. I really would appreciate more time for myself. You know we can afford it."

Her father stared, furrows building between his eyebrows. "What in heaven's name does all this have to do with Esther?"

"Maybe that's why God put us in such a good economic position, for such a time as this."

Now he regarded his daughter with astonishment. His mouth opened and closed until he finally came out with, "Our house is getting rather full. Don't they have a child? Where would they live?"

Claire rushed on, "I've been thinking about that. The whole third floor is empty. It could easily be partitioned into a parlor and two bedrooms. There's already two bathrooms up there. All one of them needs is a tub. The other one could be remodeled into a small kitchenette. The apartment wouldn't even take up the whole third floor. Wanda, their daughter, who's five, would be a wonderful companion for Eva."

Father yawned; she knew he wanted to go to bed. He knew he wouldn't win and could in fact see merit in Claire's proposal. He stood up to leave and with submission said, "Get their address. I'll write them an offer of employment in the morning."

Claire flew around the coffee table and into her father's arms. "Thank you, Daddy. I just know it will work out."

Father smiled. "It's been a long time since you've called me Daddy." With that he placed a kiss on her brow.

Chapter 16

Dear Preston,

Work on the ballroom is complete. I'm sure Jarvis is glad to stop living with Arnold in the carriage house. You should have seen Mrs. Wingate's room. There was hardly room to turn around with the extra trundle bed squeezed in for Maude and Wanda. Yesterday we worked all morning getting the room back in order.

Eva is captivated by Wanda. They have become very good friends. Poor little Eva. She said Maude looked like her mother. Jack didn't think that was true and challenged her about it. Eva admitted she was having difficulty remembering what her mother really looked like.

Since the Heaths moved to their remodeled apartment on the third floor, Eva no longer wants to sleep in the same room with Jack. She wants her own room, "just like Wanda." I could not be more pleased. Fortunately, there is still one more empty bedroom. I let Eva choose the color of paint she wanted. She said, "I want green, just like Wanda's room." Father also bought her new furniture, "just like Wanda's."

Maude and Jarvis are fitting in so well. I hadn't realized how lacking I've been in running a proper home. Father won't admit it, but he's enjoying Jarvis's ministration. Each morning his toiletry is *arranged, a clean shirt is ready, his suit is brushed and pressed and all items in his dresser are organized. He'll soon wonder how he had ever gotten along without Jarvis.*

Write soon,
Claire

Dear Sis,

This will come as a surprise but I've tried out for a play. I didn't get the lead but it's a good part. I guess I shouldn't complain since I've never acted before. I hope the whole family can come, including Aunt Charlotte!

Well, I got to get to practice.

Love,
Preston

"Are you sure Preston wants me to come? How far exactly is the college? You know I easily get tired of riding."

With an infuriated sigh, Father clenched his teeth and spoke, "Charlotte, you've traveled your whole life. It's only seventy-five miles. And yes, Preston wants you to come." Father turned to Claire, "We need to figure out who's going in which car."

"Maude and I figured that out this morning. Jarvis will drive his family, Ann, Lily, Rev. Forester, Wanda, and Eva in my car. Father please be sure to notice Eva's and Wanda's new green dresses. Maude made them. Green seems to be the new favorite color for the girls. Oh, one more thing. Jack is wearing long pants. He could use reassuring that they're right for him."

"Is Jack going with them?"

"No, he's going with us. Arnold will drive the rest of us in the Packard."

The cars pulled out of the driveway. Claire realized they were not heading in the right direction. She started to correct the chauffeur. Father stopped her, "There's another person we're taking."

Arnold turned the car into Ruth Stolon's driveway. The Pierce and the Stolon families had known each other for many years. Both families attended the same church. Claire remembered when Mr. Stolon had died. He had been in poor health for several years. Claire had relived her own mother's passing when she saw the three crying Stolon children at their father's funeral.

Claire thought, is this where Father has been going? Surely, he can't be courting her.

Father went to the door while the others waited in the cars. Ruth came out looking beautiful. She had black hair bobbed in the latest style with neat waves on each side. Her dress was black velvet. The top was an intricate beaded design starting at the neck and across the shoulders and upper arms. The beading continued down the bodice ending in a V at the midriff. The hem was fringed. She carried a fur stole. "Isn't she a bit overdressed?" remarked Aunt Charlotte.

Claire shushed her. "Don't you be shushing me, young lady!"

Father was all smiles as the couple entered the automobile.

The guests took their seats. Jack and Eva had never been to a play. Claire explained what to expect at the play. "It's like watching a story instead of reading a book. The students will be on stage pretending to be different people. You will see Preston pretending to be a soldier. It is important you are very quiet. You are not to call out to him when you see him."

A reception was held after the play. The group sat around a table drinking lemonade and discussing the play while they waited for Preston to arrive.

Father was very proud of his son. "For never having been in a play before wasn't Preston good?"

"I think he seemed to be enjoying himself. He didn't show any nervousness." This was volunteered by Maude. The other adults nodded their heads in agreement.

Claire watched Jack and Eva as they surveyed the cafeteria. "Did you enjoy the play?"

Eva was the first to respond, "Yes, I did! The ladies were dressed so pretty. I really liked the green dress that one lady had on."

Jack was more thoughtful. "Who was that girl Preston was dancing with? Couldn't she walk? You could tell he was holding her up. Why was he whispering to her? Nobody could hear what he was saying."

"I was surprised when Preston picked up the girl and started waltzing around the stage with her. Then when he came down the steps into the aisle, I think my heart skipped a beat. He could have tripped. I find it hard to believe that was part of the play. Claire, did you know he was planning to do that?"

"No, Father, I did not. I do know the girl's name is Mildred Bradberry. I really don't know much about her except she has some kind of degenerative disease."

"What does degenerative mean?" Wanda had been listening intently to the conversation.

Her father spoke up, "It means her body gets sicker as she gets older."

"Can't the doctor do something?"

"Not always."

A gentleman who knew Anthony Pierce came over to the table. "That was a startling ending to the play. Was it something that had been planned or was it an impulsive spur of the moment decision?"

"George, I was surprised as everyone else. As soon as Preston gets here, you'll find out along with the rest of us."

A somber and down-cast Preston appeared several minutes later. He sat down and took a long gulp of Claire's lemonade.

"Boy, did I ever get an ear full from the director, Miss Atkins. I thought at one point she was going to hit me. She said I'll never be in another of her plays. I really don't care."

"I take it the impromptu waltz was just that, not planned as part of the play."

Preston looked at his father and sighed, "No, Dad, it wasn't. But I felt so bad for Mildred. She didn't have a real part in the play. She was only given the part as a courtesy to her parents. They're big donors to the college. A chauffeur drives her and a nurse to her classes each day. All she did all night was sit around looking at the rest of us. So, a couple of weeks ago, I decided to try to make her feel part of the play."

Preston took another drink from Claire's glass. He watched as a tall distinguished looking gray-haired man approach the table. He was followed by a short, plump woman wrapped in a fur stole. The men at the table stood up.

"Please sit down. I'm Henry Bradberry and this is my wife, Mrs. Bradberry. We are the parents of Mildred."

Claire thought her brother was in for a second scolding. She remembered once Mrs. Wingate had told her that no good deed goes unpunished.

Henry Bradberry took Preston's hand giving it a hardy shake. "Preston, what you did tonight was so very kind and much appreciated. I don't have the words to express how grateful I am."

Mrs. Bradberry came up misty eyed and gave him a hug. She then stood on tippy toes and kissed him on his cheek. Preston stood dumbfounded. He had no response.

Mr. Pierce came to Preston's rescue, "Please sit down and have some refreshments with us."

"Thank you, but no. Mildred is in the car. We need to get her home and calm her down."

"I hope I didn't cause her any distress." Preston appeared genuinely upset as if his intended act of kindness wasn't so kind after all.

Mrs. Bradberry still held Preston's two arms, "No, no! What you did was wonderful. Picking her up and dancing around the stage and then waltzing around the aisles was amazing. This is the best thing that has ever happened to her. I will remember this evening the rest of my life. You made her so happy."

Ruth Stolon peered at Preston, "Had you practiced that with Mildred? Did she know you were going to pick her up and dance with her?"

"I only told her to be prepared for something special. I said that at the end of the play I was going to approach her with a surprise. I practiced with another girl, and Prof. Kingsly, the orchestra director. We came over early several mornings before anyone else was here. Prof. Kingsly played the piano as we practiced."

Claire hoped Professor Kingsly wouldn't be in trouble, too.

Chapter 17

The December weather had been variable. The temperature would be in the high sixties one day and the next below freezing.

Dale Gault was driving home from the police station when he spied Jack walking slowly home. He was dragging his feet like he didn't have a friend in the world. Dale pulled over and tooted his horn. Jack saw him and a big smile lit up his face as he ran to the car.

Dale leaned across the seat and opened the passenger door. "Hop in, Jack. What are you doing walking home so late? Do you want a ride?"

"Thanks, Mr. Gault. Miss Brighty made me stay after school because she said I was inappropriate. I don't even know what that means."

"It means you did something wrong or unacceptable."

"All I did was yell 'hi' to a friend I saw getting a drink out in the hall."

"Teachers must keep order in the classroom. They can't be allowing students to yell out anytime they want to. Perhaps tomorrow you should talk to your teacher. You don't want to have any bad feelings between the two of you."

By this time, they had arrived at the Pierce residence. Rev. Forester's car was in the driveway. Dale recognized the car and his heart sank.

"The preacher's here. Want to come in?"

"No, not this time. I don't want to intrude."

"What's that mean?"

"It means I need to get on home."

One morning five days before Christmas, Father came into the dining room.

 Claire had just finished feeding Adrian his breakfast. He was banging a spoon on his high chair making Eva laugh.

"My goodness, what a racket! Can you quiet them? I need a word with you."

"Eva, wash your face. Ann, please take Adrian. Thank you. What is it, Father?"

Before saying more, Father poured himself a cup of coffee. Taking a slice of toast, he slowly covered it with a thick amount of strawberry jam and cut it into two pieces. He set it on his plate without taking a bite or a drink of coffee. Claire was getting antsy with this drawn-out delay. Why didn't he get on with whatever it was he wanted to say?

"As you may have surmised, Ruth and I have become quite fond of each other. Last Wednesday, I asked her to marry me and she accepted. She would like to be married in May."

Claire sat thunderstruck. She sat as if frozen, her mind going in a thousand directions at once. She had suspicioned this might happen, but not so soon. Now what? She feared the changes. With much effort she smiled at her father, "I must confess this is not much of a surprise. I've felt for some time you two were falling in love. Congratulations, I'm happy for you."

"Love, what an interesting word. I never thought I could love anyone but your mother. I've been so lonely for the type of companionship that exists between a husband and wife. You are truly happy for me?"

Claire got up and walked around the table to her father. She put her arms around his shoulders and gave him a kiss on his cheek. "Yes, I am truly happy for you. Thank you for telling me first."

"You realize this is going to necessitate a great many changes? And that is what we must talk about."

"I realize that. What can I do to help?" Apparently, this was to be her lot in life, helping facilitate changes.

"I've invited Ruth and her three children to lunch Saturday. I thought a casual gathering would be better than a formal dinner. Preston, Cecilia, and your Aunt Charlotte need to be here also. Please see to the task. They plan to arrive at one." Father smiled at Claire, got up and left without ever having touched his breakfast.

Claire crossed her arms, clenched her teeth, and scowled. What information had he given? Nothing! That was the way it had been for fifteen years, ever since Mother's death. Father just left her to "see to the task." She was furious. How did he consider seeing to the task as learning about what was to change?

However, it did no good to stew. A lesson she had learned long ago. No matter how much it angered her, she might just as well see to the task.

Saturday morning Claire helped Jack and Eva dress. Jack didn't want to attend. Eva was very excited. Claire instructed the children how to behave.

"Who are these kids that are coming?"

"Jack! They are young people. Nigel is Mrs. Stolen's older son. He goes to the same college as Preston."

"Are they friends?"

"Friends? Well, I don't believe they associate with the same people at college. So, they're not exactly friends."

"What's associate mean?" asked Eva as she flounced about in her green dress.

"It means to do things together." Claire continued. "Eunice is Mrs. Stolon's daughter. She is sixteen and attends a private girls' academy." Eva turned towards Claire. Before Eva could ask Claire said, "An academy is a school. Eunice lives there during the school year. She only comes home on holidays and in the summer."

"Just like Preston?"

"Yes, like Preston. Edward is eleven, the youngest. He goes to a private military school. You might become good friends with him, Jack."

"I doubt it. I heard Cecilia talking on the phone. She said Eunice thinks she's better then she really is. And Edward is a pimple." Eva put her hands over her mouth and giggled.

"Jack! That is enough. I expect both of you to be on your best behavior, no matter how anyone else behaves. Now, I hear people talking. Let's go find out what's going on." Claire and the children came down the stairs and into the dining room.

"Lily, remove those two place settings." Lily stood like a statue, not sure what to do.

"Good afternoon, Mrs. Stolon. I'm sorry I didn't hear you come in. Are your children here? May I ask why you are asking for the place settings to be removed?"

"It isn't proper for Jack and Eva to attend. They are much too young to be eating with the adults. My son is driving his sister and brother here. They will arrive shortly."

Claire was shocked into silence. She didn't want to create a scene. But isn't that exactly what this woman was doing?

And wasn't Edward just one year older than Jack?

Father was standing by the buffet. He bit his lip before responding. "Perhaps just this once it might be better for the children to eat in the kitchen."

Claire couldn't believe what he had just said. Father was siding with this woman. Claire didn't know Ruth well. The infrequent times they had socialized, she had admired Ruth's manner and deportment, although she was very formal and correct. She was kind and worked in several church activities. Was Ruth now showing her true colors?

Ruth gave the children a patronizing smile, "You won't mind eating in the kitchen, will you?"

Jack looked at each person then at Claire. He grabbed Eva's arm and as he dragged her to the kitchen door he replied, "No. It'll be better than sitting in a stuffy old dining room." Ruth gave Claire a look of censure. Claire realized, because of the children's background, Ruth probably thought them as low class or aberrant.

Claire behaved politely as she had told the children to. Inside she was seething. The changes were already beginning.

Mrs. Wingate outdid herself serving a splendid meal. No one even asked to have the salt or pepper passed. Innocuous, polite conversation was discussed around the table about upcoming plans for Christmas in two days.

The group proceeded to the front parlor for coffee and cookies. An obvious uncomfortable tension permeated the room. No one took any cookies. Claire thought, Good! The children will like them. They were Mrs. Wingate's meticulously decorated Christmas cookies.

Father finally broke the tension, "Well, there is much we need to discuss. I've been thinking what is the best way to go about it. First, Ruth will be selling her house. We will all be living here."

Before he could continue, Aunt Charlotte spoke, "I've seen this coming for some time. Therefore, I've taken it upon myself to make new arrangements." Everyone looked at her with varying degrees of surprise and misgiving. "For the last several weeks I've been spending a good deal of time at the doll house. Trudy, Olivia, and I get along very well. I've even been giving Trudy piano lessons. She is quite good. Anthony, with your permission and a bit of makeover at the cottage, I would like to move in with them. Olivia and I have already discussed it and she agrees."

Claire couldn't have been more surprised if Aunt Charlotte had said she was going to be taking up field hockey. "Is there room for you in that house?"

"With some rearranging, yes. All the bedrooms are on the upper level. Olivia said they have never used the dining room since moving in. I can use that as my bedroom. I think the butler's pantry could be converted to a bathroom without undo expense."

Father beamed with pleasure, "That sounds like an excellent decision. I'll get started on the arrangements right after the holidays!"

"I'm glad you agree. Now, I promised the children we would go for a walk. Good afternoon, all." As Charlotte said this, she rose and walked out of the room with her back straight and her head held high.

Rearranging her skirt, Ruth spoke, "I think the next thing that we must consider is the staff." She looked at her fiancé for support.

"You're right. Mrs. Wingate prepared a pleasing meal and she is a wonderful cook. However, Ruth's cook is a French trained professional chef."

"Yes, Gabin has been with me for over fifteen years. I don't want to lose him. I want him to take over the duties here. I don't mean to put Mrs. Wingate out. She could continue under Gabin. She makes lovely desserts. These beautiful Christmas cookies are testimony to that culinary skill. And perhaps considering her age, she might appreciate less work."

Claire stared at her father. She had no words.

Father eyed Claire but came to Ruth's rescue. "Ruth likes to entertain more than we have been doing. I think two cooks could work out well. Don't you, Claire?" He almost pleaded with her to agree.

She wanted to be honest even though she thought she was in a losing battle. "It will be difficult to make such an adjustment. Mrs. Wingate has also been with us for several years. She may feel humiliated and think she is being considered inadequate."

"I realize it is a delicate situation. And must be handled carefully and with tack.

But we won't find out how she will respond until we announce the change, will we?" Ruth gave Claire a sweet smile as she continued, "My housekeeper is elderly. Her brother-in-law recently passed away. Her sister has asked her to move to Virginia to live with her. Your housekeeper, what is her name, again, please?"

Claire and Father spoke up at the same time, "Maude."

"Yes, Maude is her name. I'd like her to stay. However, George my butler is professionally trained. I understand yours is not."

Before Ruth could continue, Anthony interrupted, "There will be no problem with that. Jarvis and I have had several discussions." He glanced at Claire, "You know he spends as much time in the green house as he can. The place was in shambles before he started working on it. He repaired the window tiles and cleaned out all the debris from the beds. You should see it. He actually has things growing!

"He was raised to work in his family's truck garden business. His mother had a large flower garden besides the family vegetable garden. Jarvis really knows a great deal about plants, lawns, and such. He has agreed to take over the responsibility as head gardener. I think he is really looking forward to the position."

Ruth ignored what Father had just said and continued. "As to the maids' positions, I have a personal maid who of course, will come with me. Also in my employment are three additional maids, the parlor maid, an upstairs maid, and a laundress. Oh, there are two girls in the kitchen to help

Gabin. With so many in the family, I feel we can keep your two girls in addition to mine." Ruth hardly paused to take a breath. "Next, we need to discuss the living arrangements for everyone."

On the outside, Claire sat with her hands in her lap and looked relaxed. On the inside, she was trying desperately not to panic. She had no control over anything. She had no say, in any of the changes. Did she even have a place in this house anymore? What about the children? What were Ruth's plans for them? Was Ruth expecting to move into Claire's mother's apartment that she and Adrian now occupied? After all, it did connect to her father's rooms.

Nigel, Ruth's son, spoke, "Before you continue, Mother, I want to say something."

"Yes. What is it?"

"You don't have to be concerned about my living arrangements. I'm getting married next Friday, the twenty-eight."

Ruth looked at her son and gasped, "What do you mean you are getting married! You most certainly are not! You have another semester of college. And we talked about a tour of Europe for you."

"Those plans have changed." Nigel stood. He appeared shy and uncomfortable as he surveyed the room. He gave a deep slow sigh before continuing, "It is expedient that we get married."

By now Ruth was angry, "Expedient!" Then the reason dawned on her. "Who is the girl?"

"Her name is Henrietta Martin. She's the chaplain's daughter."

Preston, who had been quietly listening to the goings on grunted, "So you're the one."

Anthony gave his son a censuring severe look, "Preston, be quiet. Please continue, Nigel. What are your plans?"

"We're having a small ceremony at the minister's house Friday evening. Until I can get a job and a place for us to live, Rev. Martin said we could stay with them."

"What about your schooling? You only have one semester left. Five months! You can't quit now!"

"Calm down, Ruth. This is something that needs to be discussed privately. We'll talk about it later." Father gave Nigel a sympathetic gaze.

Ruth bit her lip and glowered at her son. She then squared her shoulders and continued. Claire couldn't believe what she was hearing Ruth say. She planned to send Jack to the military school her son attended! Had Ruth and Anthony already talked about this? Next, Ruth told the group she wanted to use Trudy's old bedroom suite, the one Cecilia now called hers, to use as a nursery and hire a nanny.

Cecilia jumped to her feet, "No you can't do that! Those are mine!" She turned to squarely face her father. "Father, you can't let her do that!"

Before he could reply, Ruth continued with her plans, "Cecilia, I have something better in mind. I would like you to go to 'Miss Jennifer's Boarding School for Young Ladies.' It is the one Eunice attends."

"I'm not going to some old stuffy boarding school!" Cecilia looked again at her father for help. "Father, I have my friends here. I don't want to leave them. I'll be all alone."

"It's not stuffy! It's a very nice school where one learns manners and to do as their elders tell them. And you sure will be all alone because nobody would want to be your friend anyway." Ruth's daughter, Eunice, yelled across the room at Cecilia.

Anthony raised his hand to quiet the girls. "You two, sit down." He frowned at Ruth. "This isn't going very well, is it? We'll table that decision until we have explored all the possibilities."

Quietly Claire spoke, "Jack is doing so well in school. He has made several friends. For the first time he is finding stability. Sending him away will cause him to think he has once again been abandoned. And what's wrong with my continuing to look after the children? Am I not doing an adequate job?"

"Claire, I think I've just thought of a better plan," Father stood and moved close to Claire. He took her right hand in both of his, "My Dear, how would you like your own home? I could lease a house for you and the children. You can take Mrs. Wingate and even Ann with you. I'll see that you are given a monthly income for expenses. I probably will have to remain the guardian of the children. However, you don't have to let anyone know that."

Ruth clapped her hands, "Anthony, that's wonderful. What a marvelous idea! If you moved to another town where you're not known, you could let people believe you're a widow and the children your own."

Claire weighed what Father and Ruth had just said. This woman was evil! Was Father blind? Ruth's words were sucking the air from the room. Claire's insides were tight.

She thought she might throw-up. Would Father agree for her to live a lie the rest of her life? Getting up she whispered, "Excuse me, I need to leave."

As she hurried out of the room, she heard Cecelia start in again about her objections to giving up her apartment and going off to school. Claire covered her ears and ran.

Chapter 19

Rushing toward the door, Claire grabbed a coat from the hall closet and left the house. Dark clouds hung in the air. A slight breeze harassed her hair. Aimlessly she walked from one street to another, turning corners with no thought of where she was going.

It was two days before Christmas. Last minute shoppers were numerous. Some recognized Claire and greeted her. At first, she tried to be pleasant and return a "Merry Christmas," to each one. Her distress at giving pleasant responses when she was anything but merry was so great, she finally gave up and ignored the greetings.

Logical reasoning told her, her father was trying to help. She still heard Ruth's voice in her head saying she just wanted her and the children out of the way.

Yes, allowing her father to lease a house and give her a monthly income might be the best. She would be mistress of her own place. The practical side of the issue had possibilities. And what difference would it make if people thought her a widow?

She couldn't get past the feeling of being a kept woman. It stabbed at her heart. Is that what she had been all her life?

Rain fell, gentle at first. Then harder. The rain turned to a sleet as the temperature dropped. Claire was soon soaked and cold. She realized she had only put on a light cloth coat. It was no match for the sleet and snow now starting. She wasn't sure where she was until she saw the spiral from the First Presbyterian Church at the edge of downtown. Music could be heard from the inside. A choir must be practicing for their Christmas program. It drew her.

Claire gazed across the lawn and saw a softly lit nativity scene. Near the church the wise men with their camels arrived. Closer to the creche two shepherds with several sheep stood guard. In the center lay the baby Jesus in a wooden manger. Joseph protectively stood over Him. Mary knelt beside her Son.

It bothered Claire that Mary was usually portrayed this way. Would a woman who had just given birth be kneeling. Well, what did she know? She had never had a baby and probably never would.

Claire stared at the Virgin. "All my life it seems I've been doing for others, first, caring for Cecilia, Trudy and even Preston. I'm the only mother Cecilia knows. Now there's Jack, Eva, and Adrian. I've tried to do what's best for them and put myself last. I want someone to care about me. I don't want to always be the one expected to give."

Claire's mind wandered to thoughts of the Christmas story, "Mary, you did everything right. You were the most blessed of all women. Yet look at all the trouble you went through."

Long forgotten words of her mother returned to Claire, "Being a Christian and living in God's will, is not a guarantee against troubles or sorrows. We are promised God's comfort and that our lives will have meaning. Whatever God allows you to go through is for your benefit."

"Please, God, help me. I love you, Jesus, show me what to do." She stood staring at the nativity and felt a Presence, *"What if things don't turn out the way you want them to? Are you willing to place your life in My hands to do as I know is best for you?"*

"Yes, God. I give You my life to do as You choose. If it would please You, I really want a husband to love and the children to be my own."

Claire was oblivious to the traffic noise behind her as she stood shivering in front of the church. Something warm draped over her shoulders. She turned to find the kind person and gazed into the concerned face of Lieutenant Dale Gault.

"Claire? What are you doing standing here in this storm? You didn't hear me honking my horn? You're not even dressed suitable for such weather." Tears streamed down her face. She shook her head but said nothing.

Dale gently put his arm around her and walked her to his car. After getting her seated in the passenger side, he reached into his back seat and retrieved a blanket. Apparently, his car had no heater. He wrapped the blanket snuggly around Claire being careful to cover her cold legs and feet.

He got in the driver's seat and guided his car out into the Christmas traffic. Dale had to drive vigilantly. The snow-covered roads were treacherous. Reckless pedestrians darted here and there. He couldn't help but look intermittently at Claire. Neither one spoke until he turned the car into a long driveway.

At the end of the driveway was a dark three-story house. A large snow-covered lawn was separated by a wide sidewalk. On either side of the walkway were large leafless maple trees. Surrounding the house were several evergreen bushes. Oddly, Claire's first thought was that this home must really be pretty in the summer. Then she had another thought! Claire spoke for the first time, "Where are you taking me?"

Dale continued up the driveway to the back of the house. The rear part of the house radiated soft lights onto the fallen snow. "This is my house."

"I can't go in there! I have enough problems without someone seeing me go into a man's house."

Dale chuckled, "It's alright. My grandma lives with me. And our neighbor is probably still here. She comes over a couple of times a week to cook and clean." He parked the car and went over to the passenger side to help Claire into the house.

"Well, what have you brought home to us today?" A tall, thin elderly woman sat at a kitchen table slicing potatoes. She sounded as if bringing a stranger into the house was a regular occurrence. Across from her was her opposite, a short, plump, middle-aged woman. Where the older woman was pale with gnarled hands, the younger woman was rosy cheeked, wearing an assortment of rings.

"Grandma, this is Claire Pierce. Claire, this is my grandma, Mrs. Louise Gault, and this is our neighbor, Joyce Murry." Claire stood by the back door not sure what to do or say.

"Oh, my goodness, Dear. I've been wanting to meet you for the longest time! I admire you so much. But look at you. You're soaked and cold. You look like a drowned kitten!" As Grandma spoke, she painfully got out of her chair and started giving instructions. "Joyce, go into my room and find some undergarments and something else for this poor child. Look in my bottom bureau drawer. Dale, make some hot chocolate. Come, Sweet, we must get you out of these wet things."

Grandma propelled Claire into a pleasant sitting room off the kitchen. It was warm and cozy. An electric heater sat inside a small fireplace. Grandma turned the heater up. Two couches faced each other in front of the fireplace. On the opposite side of the room were three large windows with the drapes closed likely to help keep in the heat. The hardwood floor was covered by an old and badly warn Persian rug. At one time it must had been bright blue.

Grandma continued to lead Claire into an ornate bathroom. Even in Claire's distress, she couldn't help but admire the decor. The walls and tile were white except for one wall. A beautiful oriental scene was painted on that wall. The woodwork around the bathroom window had also been adorned with an oriental motif. This bathroom was amazing. Was someone in the family an artist? Was it Dale?

Joyce followed the two ladies into the bathroom. She and Grandma set to work drying Claire. They wrapped some sort of turban around her head. No one said much. Claire was amazed at their proficiency. Warm cashmere underwear, much too big, showed up next. Grandma skillfully pinned the underwear around Claire. Next Grandma slipped a lace trimmed silk chamise over her head. Lastly, she was told to hold up her arms. She was helped into a soft wool dress with alternating narrow dark brown and yellow stripes. It was much out of fashion but very warm. Claire was too tired and confused by all that had happened to be concerned about modesty.

Grandma stood back and looked at her creation. "The dress is much too long. Joyce, get a belt. We can pull up some of the skirt and belt it. She also needs socks and shoes. See what you can find."

They returned to the sitting room once Grandma was satisfied with the job. Claire was led to a much-used velvet covered couch and directed to sit. Soon Dale came in carrying a tray with cups and a plate of cookies. Grandma smiled at her grandson, "We'll leave you two to your business." Grandma and Joyce returned to the kitchen, closing the door between the two rooms.

Lieutenant Gault was skilled in getting people to disclose their problems. He decided the best way to get Claire to talk was to first tell her about his family. He sat across from Claire, smiled and offered her the chocolate and a cookie. "I suppose you can't help but wonder about all this." He lifted his hands and spread his fingers. "This house originally belonged to my grandparents. My grandpa was a physician. The front of the house, which we seldom use, besides having the normal front and back parlors and dining room, has a patient waiting room, exam room and office. Upstairs are a bunch of bedrooms. A couple of the bedrooms were used as overnight hospital rooms for patients needing extra care.

"My dad was also a doctor. My grandma is a trained nurse. In January of 1902 my dad was out on an emergency call. He slipped on some ice, fracturing his skull. He died three days later. I was just six." He stopped talking and looked into his cup as if remembering the event. After several seconds he relaxed his shoulders and continued.

"My mom and I moved into this house with my grandparents. An aunt also lived here. All of us worked together as a team helping Grandpa. I got the job of looking after the well children when they came along with their mothers. I'm really pretty good at babysitting." Dale smiled as if remembering.

"It was the dream of my grandpa to have me follow him. Truthfully, I didn't want to hurt his feelings but I wasn't real interested in being a doctor. So, I decided to join the Army and decide about medical school later. Then the influenza hit in 1916. First, my Aunt Erma got it and died. Then it took my mom. I tried to get out of the Army but by then the Great War was on and the U.S. was soon in it. My grandpa died while I was in France." Once again Dale stopped. He looked at Claire with such sad eyes, it made her heart ache.

Dale took a sip of the now cooled chocolate and continued. "Finally, I got out of the Army and got home. I learned my grandfather had left me this house and all his money. It was with the understanding that I take care of Grandma. That's what we've been doing ever since, looking out for each other. She lives in these rooms. I've fixed up a couple of rooms upstairs for me. Joyce comes in to clean and cook us some meals."

Both sat quietly absorbed in his and her own thoughts. Dale cocked his head to one side, "I've told you, my story. Do you feel up to telling me why you were standing in a snow storm crying?"

Claire looked at Dale. A tear lay on Claire's lower eye lid, finally trickling down her cheek. This was followed by one down her other cheek. Then a stream of tears cascaded down her face and out her nose.

She felt Dale sit beside her and his arm around her shoulders. Then he put his handkerchief in her hand. Oh, this is what Claire wanted, someone to care about her. To truly care. His arm felt so comforting around her. She didn't want him to let her go.

Dale was thinking, this is what he wanted, to hold Claire forever. He wanted her to be his for the rest of their lives. She felt so good in his arms.

After the release of her anguish, Claire straightened up, blew her nose, and deeply sighed. 'My father and a lady from our church, Ruth Stolon, are getting married. She will be mistress of the house and has voiced several things she wants to change."

Dale eyed her skeptically. "What do you mean by change?"

Claire put her hand over her mouth and again sighed through her fingers. "She's suggesting several changes with the household staff. Worse, she wants Jack to go to military school and to hire a nanny for Eva and Adrian."

Again, she stopped. This time she lifted her head and despondently regarded Dale. "My father offered an alternative. He will lease a house for the children and me. Ruth suggested that I pretend I'm a widow."

She made two fist and declared, with obstinate agony, "I want to be their mother. But I don't want to live a lie the rest of my life and be a kept woman."

Dale rose and walked to the fireplace staring into the glowing electric heater. "I don't understand. If you're going to marry

Rev. Forester, can't the two of you then adopt the children?"

"Rev. Forester? Who said I was going to marry him?"

"He did. I saw him coming out of Ehrenberg's Jewelry Store this morning. He showed me a ring set that he'd picked up. He said he'd just had it sized and was getting married."

Claire's eyes sparkled and a smile replaced her sad countenance. Blessed laughter poured out of her. "It's not me he's marrying. It's Lily!"

"Lily? Your maid?"

"Yes. He's been courting her ever since he arrived last spring. She'll make a wonderful minister's wife. She knows all about entertaining and pleasing people."

"Do you mean all the times I drove by your house and saw his car in the driveway, he was visiting Lily?"

"I didn't know you drove by our house so frequently."

"Well, I just wanted to be sure everything was all right." Dale began to pace back and forth in front of the fireplace. To Claire's astonishment, he suddenly moved to her. He got down on one knee taking both her hands in his. "Marry me."

Claire's eyes opened wide, not believing what she had just heard Dale say. "What did you say?"

"I said, will you marry me? Claire, I think I've been in love with you from that first morning I saw you coming into that ground floor dining room. Please marry me. We can adopt the children. I told you that I have a lot of experience caring for kids. Even if I didn't, I'd still want to marry you and be their father."

Hardly taking a breath, Dale continued, "This is a big house; it's huge. There are eight bedrooms upstairs. Each of the kids could have their own room. You can decorate and remodel the place anyway you want. And if you don't like this house, I'll sell it and buy you another."

Dale was now down on both knees and holding Claire's hands so tight, they were beginning to hurt. Each looked deeply into the other's eyes. Then the telephone rang.

Chapter 20

"That blasted phone! Sometimes I wish it hadn't been invented." Dale rose and went to a small desk next to the door leading to his grandma's bedroom. Much too robustly he answered, "Hello!" He listened while the caller talked then, intermittently replied, "What? All of them? How long? She's here with me. We're on our way!"

By now Claire was standing. "What is it?" All thought of romance was gone.

"Your Aunt Charlotte, Trudy and the children are missing. We must get over to your house." Wrapping an arm around

Claire's waist and taking her elbow, he led her into the kitchen. He grabbed Joyce's coat hanging on a peg by the back door and wrapped it around her. He almost chuckled because it was big enough to go around her twice.

"Grandma, we've got a call from the station. Claire's kids and her aunt are missing. We're headed over to her place."

Claire, although fighting back panic, couldn't help but notice Dare called the children her kids.

It was a treacherous journey to the Pierce house. Snow continued to come down and the Christmas traffic was heavy. Several cars were in ditches. One had unsuccessfully tried to move a hundred-year- old oak tree. The tree had won. The driver was standing in ankle deep snow surveying a damaged right fender.

Dale turned the car into the snow-covered circle drive of the Pierce home. Every light in the house appeared to be on. Several police cars lined the driveway. Because of the driving snow, policemen were barely visible walking around the grounds. Mrs. Wingate's daughter, Maude, met them at the front door.

"Claire, something has happened to the children and your aunt. They went for a walk and haven't returned. Now it's getting dark and they should be home. Mr. Pierce, Preston, and Jarvis are out looking for them." Maude began to cry. "I'm so scared. What if that awful man got out of jail somehow and is back?"

Dale had been discussing the situation with the police officers present and heard Maude's remark. "Let me assure you, Mrs. Heath, Buck Smith is still in jail. He has nothing to do with this. We'll find the children. Probably, Claire's aunt decided to stop someplace dry and safe to wait out the storm." He wasn't sure he believed this and neither did Maude.

"Then why hasn't she or someone called to let us know where they are?"

There was a great deal of commotion at the back stairway. Jack came running into the foyer. He was covered in mud and his coat had a tear down the left sleeve. On the left side of his forehead was a large noticeable purple bump. A police officer followed him holding a blanket. With chagrin the officer looked at Dale and said, "Sorry sir, I tried to wrap him up. He just moved too fast."

Jack ran over to Claire tugging at her to come with him, "We need help! The floor fell in and we were trapped in the bottom!

Aunt Charlotte is caught under some boards. Wanda's arm is hurt. I was the only one that could climb out. Trudy helped me get out."

Claire beseechingly fixed her eyes on Dale. He knelt in front of Jack, "Son, you need to slow down. Start from the beginning and tell us what happened."

Before Jack could retell his story, Mr. Pierce and Preston came through the front door. "We heard Jack has been found." Mr. Pierce babbled as if he might faint. Dale quickly got up and propelled Mr. Pierce to a side chair forcing him to sit.

He then told Jack to take a deep breath and explain what happened.

Jack breathed in deeply, then with wide eyes looked around at the group and told his story, "We were walking home through the short cut in the woods. It started raining. Aunt Charlotte said she knew a place we could go to wait until the rain stopped. She took us to an old house. Some of the roof was missing. We all went in and headed to a corner where there was still some roof. All of a sudden, the floor broke! We all ended up in a big hole." The boy tugged at Dale, "Come on. They need help."

"I know where the place is. My friends and I used to play in there when we were kids." Preston motioned as he started out the door.

Claire watched as Dale and other police followed Preston. Jack shivering and dripping wet wanted to go. Claire looked at him, "No. You need to get out of those clothes and get warmed up. Ann, go to

Jack's room and get pajamas, his robe, and slippers. Oh, get some socks too."

Claire took Jack into her suite, wrapped a blanket around him and told him to undress. Ann came in with his night clothes. With Jack still wrapped in the blanket, she told him to dress. When he was finished, Claire nodded, "That will do for now. Let's get you fed."

They entered the dining room and stood amazed. The table was decked out with sliced ham, roast beef, bread, rolls, fruit and vegetable salads, as well as several hot side dishes. On one end were piled plates, silverware, and napkins. On the buffet sat three fruit pies, two cream pies, two cakes, cookies, and a large coffee pot.

Claire stared at Mrs. Wingate, who was putting cups by the coffee pot, "Isn't this the food we've been preparing for Christmas Eve and dinner on Christmas Day?"

Mrs. Wingate chuckled at Claire's surprise. "I know those policemen and the other helpers are going to be hungry. They deserve to have food ready. We'll just have to make do later. By the way, why are you dressed like that?"

Claire was embarrassed. So worried about the children and her aunt, she had totally forgotten about her appearance.

Chapter 21

Preston followed by Dale and six policemen, hurried down an obscure path through woods behind the Pierce home. The men carried a ladder, rope, and blankets. It was almost dark and difficult going. Preston had a challenge staying on the trail. Jack's footprints had already disappeared due to the snow.

"Hold up. Preston. Officer McCrae has fallen." Dale used his flashlight to examine the policeman.

"I'm all right, Sir."

"No, you're not. It looks like you've broken your arm. Head back to the house."

As McCrae trudged back toward the house disappearing into the falling snow, Dale thought to yell, "Call for an ambulance."

Preston hadn't waited as Dale had asked. Out of the darkness, he heard Preston yell, "There it is!"

The log cabin was partially collapsed. Much of the chinking between the logs was missing and most of the wood shingles on the remaining roof were also gone. All the glass from the windows was broken or missing. The front door hung on one hinge.

Out loud, Preston wondered, "Whatever possessed my aunt to take the kids in there?"

Trudy called from the dark hole. The rescuers got down on their knees and peered over the edge. Several flashlights shined into what appeared to have been a large root cellar. "Preston, is that you? Help us! Aunt Charlotte is caught under some boards. And Wanda's arm is bent funny. She's been crying. We can't get out."

Dale shouted, "Stay still, we'll get you out." The flashlights scanned the hole. They saw Eva and Wanda huddled together near Aunt Charlotte whose left leg was covered by a heavy log. All three were sitting in muddy water up to their waists. Trudy stood in water near the dirt wall looking up at the men.

"Lower the ladder." Before Dale had a chance to send anyone down, Trudy started up. Preston helped her over the edge. She gave him a big hug.

This surprised him. He didn't think she liked him.

Dale beckoned to a young officer, "Wrap that blanket around her and take her back to the house. Let's get down there and get the others out."

Policemen started climbing into the hole. Dale informed them, "Officer Wolfe served with the ambulance corps during the war and has first-aid training. Let him see to Wanda. It is obvious her arm is broken."

Wolfe secured Wanda's arm to her chest and gently carried her up the ladder. He instructed another officer to take her back to the house, showing him how to carry her.

"Help me up! I want to go with Wanda." Eva was struggling to stand. Once up, she insisted on climbing the ladder without anyone helping her. Wrapped in a blanket, she allowed a policeman to carry her back to the house.

All during this time, Dale, Preston and two policemen had been working on freeing Aunt Charlotte. "This log is not only large but water soaked. Preston put your arms around your aunt while we lift the log off her leg." She gave a sigh and leaned into Preston's chest. As the log gave way, Charlotte fainted.

Wolfe looked at her and stated, "It's okay that she fainted. We'll be able to move her and she won't feel the pain." He examined the leg. "I don't think it's fractured. Just the same I'll splint it before we move her. That will ease any pain she is likely to experience."

Charlotte's eyes opened wide as Wolfe was working on her leg. At first, she didn't seem to be aware of the environs. Realizing what had happened and where she was, she looked over her shoulder at Preston and again relaxed.

Charlotte was not a small woman. It took tactful maneuvering to get her up the ladder. She did not complain even though each jostling of her body sent a pain through her leg.

Once out of the cellar, there was several minutes of discussion as the best way to carry her back to the house. It was agreed that two officers would make a chair by putting their arms together. This necessitated them to walk sideways. A difficult task through the snow.

An ambulance was waiting for them at the house. Jarvis had returned from his search. He was in the ambulance holding Wanda. Charlotte was put on a stretcher and into the ambulance. Anthony rode with his sister to the hospital. All the policemen and other helpers were preparing to leave.

Claire came outside. "Gentlemen, please stay for a bite to eat. Everything is ready. Don't be concerned about your boots. Just come in."

"Miss, that's very kind of you. We've been down in that hole and are filthy."

"No, Miss. Clarence is right. Look at my uniform. It's caked with mud."

Claire responded, "A workman is worth his pay. Please. Come in."

A third officer spoke, "Well, where can we wash up?"

An hour later all had left. Mrs. Wingate and the rest of the household scanned the nearly empty table.

Cecilia shook her head and pouted, "The food was for tomorrow night and our Christmas dinner. What are we going to do?"

Don't worry, we'll be okay. Getting the little ones and your Aunt Charlotte back was more important." Mrs. Wingate smiled at Cecilia. "Right now, I'm tired. We'll see what we can do in the morning for our meals."

Father, Jarvis, and Wanda returned home later that evening.

Wanda had a broken arm. She sleepily showed off her white cast. Before being carried to her bedroom she informed everyone, "The doctor told me to get as many people as I can to sign my cast. He said the last person he put a cast on got ninety-two autographs. I told him I could do more than that!"

Father explained to the waiting family, "Aunt Charlotte only has a sprained ankle. However, because of her age, the doctor decided to keep her overnight as a precaution."

Chapter 22

Christmas Eve day dawned clear and cold. Claire was putting the final touches on the Christmas tree. She heard Eva and Wanda scamper down the stairs.

Eva stopped in the doorway, "Oh Miss, those things are so pretty. They shine like silver. What are they called?" Wanda called Claire Miss, and Eva had taken to calling her that also. Claire didn't like it. But what was she to do?

"Eva, they're called tinsel. It represents icicles. Would you like to put some on the tree? You only put one on at a time."

Preston stood near the pocket doors watching, "Give me some of those. I'll help." He approached Claire and took a handful. Then he tossed a bunch onto the tree making the girls giggle.

Claire stamped her foot, "Preston! That's not the way to do it. Either put them on one at a time or give them back." He shrugged his shoulders and handed the icicles to Claire.

 Father came into the room, "Preston, it doesn't seem you are much help. Your Aunt Charlotte needs to be picked up from the hospital at 11:00. I have some business to finish up before lunch. You and Jack can go get her."

It was traditional to have a children's Christmas Eve service at the church. It was scheduled to begin at 7:00. Pierces planned a party after the service.

Early that evening, Aunt Charlotte sat in the parlor waiting to leave. Claire was surprised she was going. "Aunt Charlotte, are you sure you're up to going? After all the service is really for the children."

Jack piped up, before Charlotte could answer, "Aunt Charlotte must go. We have a surprise for everyone." Claire looked from Jack to her aunt. Both had coy smiles. Claire thought she saw Aunt Charlotte wink at Jack.

"I invited Policemen Gault to come!"

Surprised, Claire turned to Eva, "What! Why did you do that?"

"Because I like him. He said he would come and bring his grandma. I didn't know old people had grandmas."

"Old! How old do you think Lieutenant Gault is?"

"He must be at least twenty."

Claire did her best to hide a giggle.

The Christmas Eve service followed the usual routine. Several carols were sung, the Christmas story was read by Rev. Forester as children dressed in bathrobes and sheets acted out their parts.

Just when the congregation thought the service was about over, a table was wheeled to the center of the platform. It was covered with a white sheet under which were several lumpy objects. Rev. Forester nodded to Aunt Charlotte.

She hobbled to the front using a cane for support. She beckoned to Trudy, Jack, Eva, and Wanda. They marched to the front and stood behind the table. "Our little group has a very special surprise for you this evening. First, I must tell you a true story.

"A long time ago, England was fighting a civil war. Like the civil war we had in this country. A man by the name of Oliver Cromwell was now in charge and killing Royalists, those were people loyal to the king. A Royalist family decided to leave England for Maryland in what they referred to as the new country. Before they were able to do so, they were attacked by Cromwell's army. A maid had previously been told to sew eight silver bells in the lining of her dress. Her name was Eliza. I suppose just being a maid, the army didn't see her as a threat and she was able to run away. Eliza also had her mistress's jewelry case with her. Inside the case were the tickets for passage to Maryland

and several gold coins. There was a young man, Joseph, that she was sweet on." Charlotte smiled at this and several congregates chuckled.

"Eliza and Joseph made it to Maryland. They were married and Joseph opened a butcher shop. Eliza gave her first born daughter the bells. Down through the generations, it became a tradition for the oldest daughter to be given the bells as a wedding gift. As the various families settled in different parts of America, one of the bells was lost.

"My mother received the bells from my grandmother. When I married, I expected to be given the bells. They were not anything of great value. It was more a 'rite of passage.' However, my mother refused to give them to me. She said that I was selfish, mean and not deserving of the bells. As you can imagine I was very angry.

"I married a very nice man, Jacob Ainsworth, fifteen years my senior. I wasn't really in love with him. But he was rich. He gave me whatever my heart desired. I lacked for nothing. We had a beautiful house, servants, wonderful parties and all else that goes with wealth. After seven years of marriage my Jacob died.

"Jacob left me with enough money that it should have lasted the rest of my life. I squandered it. I bought myself jewelry. I traveled buying antiques and other trinkets. I had a private seamstress to make my clothes. Like my mother said, I was very selfish. I seldom thought of others. The gifts I bought my family were cheap and worthless."

Charlotte saw two boys start to fiddle with each other's hands. "I'd better hurry this up. Eventually I had spent all that I had. All my money was gone. Creditors took my jewelry, my house and all that was in it.

"I showed up on my brother's doorstep with everything I owned in some boxes. He and his family were so kind to me. They didn't ostracize me. They took me in and loved me. I realized just how much I had missed because of my selfishness.

"One day I was playing the piano at the stone house where Trudy lives. She was sitting beside me and said, 'That song would sound really nice on the bells.' I asked her what bells! She had found them!

"Together with Jack, Wanda, and Eva we began coming to the church after school each day to practice. I'm sure everyone has heard of our misadventure coming home from our practice yesterday." Several people laughed.

"Now we shall play *Away in a Manger* as our Christmas gift to you on Trudy's bells."

Charlotte turned to Trudy giving her a smile and a slight nod. Charlette limped to the piano bench and practically fell on it as Jack and Trudy removed the white tablecloth. Resting on the table were seven shining silver bells of various sizes. The children situated themselves behind the table. Trudy, Jack, and Wanda had two bells each. Eva had one bell. Wanda had adeptly maneuvered her second bell into her hand with the broken arm.

The children's eyes were fastened on Aunt Charlotte as she pointed to either a right hand, left hand or Eva. Each child responded by ringing his or her bell.

Charlotte struck the eighth note in the song to replace the bell that was missing.

When the song was finished, the congregation sat in silence. No one coughed, there was no shuffling of feet, and no whispering.

Rev. Forester stood, "Please stand. Let us sing this lovely carol as the children play it again for us. This will be our benediction. When the carol is finished, please quietly exit the sanctuary."

Chapter 23

Ruth Stolon and her children came to the Pierce home after the service. Dale Gault and his grandmother were also there. A light supper of tomato soup and grilled cheese sandwiches had been served. Now everyone sat in the parlor talking in small groups. All the lights in the house were out except the fire in the fireplace and the Christmas tree lights. Claire noticed Aunt Charlotte and Dale's grandmother were apparently having a serious conversation. Dale was talking to the children.

She heard Eva saying, "I asked Santa to bring me a Patsy Ann doll. And I hope he brings extra clothes for her, too."

Jack spoke up, "I asked for a Sopwith Camel windup airplane, like the ones from the war. I want to fly a real one when I grow-up!"

[Jack did not know how prophetic he was. During World War II he would pilot military transport aircraft across the Himalayan Mountains from India to China to supply the U.S. Army based in China.]

"Well, children, unless you get off to bed, Santa won't be bringing any presents to anyone." Claire stood and shepherded the children towards the door.

Dale's grandmother glanced at her grandson, "Dale, I think it's time for us to leave." With a twinkle in her eye she added, "I want to see what Santa leaves me."

After good nights and best wishes for a Merry Christmas, Claire helped Grandma Gault on with her coat.

Dale said good-bye to the children. Eva hung onto his hand. "I'll see you tomorrow. You can play with my new doll." Eva peeked at Claire and added, "I invited Mr. Gault to come over tomorrow."

"Oh, you did, did you?" This was all Claire could think of to say. She and Dale had had no time to talk alone since leaving his house. She was secretly glad Eva had done so. She chewed on her bottom lip. Her stomach quivered and her heart pounded.

Dale helped his grandmother into the car. Then he waved to Eva and Claire who stood at the open door. Claire felt a small hand in hers, "Mommie, do you think Mr. Gault would make a good daddy?"

Claire looked down at Eva's angelic face staring up through large green eyes. The child had called her Mommie. She picked Eva up and watched the Gault car disappear down the snow-covered drive. Claire kissed the little girl's nose, "Daughter I know, he will be a good daddy."

Epilog

The air was filled with wedding bells during the following six months. First, Nigel Stolon and Henrietta Martin were wed in the Martines' living room on December 30, 1928. Anthony Pierce's wedding gift was a paid six-month lease on a small apartment four blocks from the college. He also used his professional influence to secure Nigel a part-time position as a bank teller. To reach his destination required Nigel to travel by two different buses and walk the last four blocks to the bank. Mr. Pierce didn't want to make things too easy for Nigel!

Lily Lamont and Rev. Forester were the next couple to tie the knot. Lily wanted to be married on St. Valentine's Day, which fell Thursday that year. The church was filled with relatives, friends, and congregants. Lily shocked most of the older women and delighted the younger ones by having attendants, Claire and Ann, wear bright red dresses. Claire knew she would never wear her dress again. Maude made gorgeous red dresses for the girls' dolls.

The next couple to marry were Ruth Stolon and Anthony Pierce. They chose May 4th, 1929, as their wedding day. The marriage was celebrated in the newly renovated Pierce's flower garden created by Javis Heath. Half way through the service

Henrietta went in to labor and had to leave for the hospital. That evening while all the guests enjoyed a lavish French meal, Ruth became a grandmother to a lovely baby girl.

Ruth's children stayed at their respective private schools. Cecilia was allowed to keep her suite of rooms and continue at the public school.

The last wedding of the year was that of Claire and Dale on June 22, 1929. Claire found her mother's wedding gown that had been carefully packed in a trunk. The white, 1890's garment was satin with yards and yards of Belgian lace, mutton sleeves and a bustle.

Maude skillfully disassembled the dress. Using a picture of a Chanel wedding dress she'd seen in a magazine, she refashioned it into a chic 1929 gown. Claire's mother's head piece was a wide brimmed hat made of satin. Satin roses covered the top with a cluster of white feathers. Maude removed the brim. She then covered the cap with lace and attached a lace veil and train. The roses were sewn in a cluster at the left edge of the cap.

After Maude and Ann had helped Claire get ready for the service, she asked to be alone for a few minutes. She rested on a short sofa as she looked out the window and pondered all the events that had taken place over the past twelve months. Only God knew what the rest of 1929, and beyond would hold. She would trust Him. There was a soft knock at her door, "Come in."

Aunt Charlotte entered looking fabulous in a violet chiffon garment. Trudy followed her dressed in a shimmering rose gown. Charlotte stepped to one side and let Trudy go past her. Trudy smiled as she walked across the room to Claire. In her hands was a box covered haphazardly in white tissue paper. She sat down next to Claire and handed her the box. "This is my gift to you." Claire took the box and looked at Trudy then Charlotte. "Well open it, Claire. Don't you want to see what I'm giving you? And it's just for you. Not that guy."

"Do you mean Dale? He's going to be your brother."

"I know! I know! Who cares. Open your present."

Claire carefully unwrapped the box. In it were seven silver bells. "Trudy, these are yours."

Trudy gave Claire a loving smile, "I want you to have them. Then when your daughter gets married, you give them to her."

The End

Acknowledgments

Thank you to the following for their invaluable advice and help writing this book: Jennifer Cary, Dana Keifer, Linda Barr, Timothy Pester, and the wonderful ladies at Typewriter Creative Co.

Books by Marsha Pester

Secret Circumstance

Secret Skeleton

Secret of What Matters Most

www.ingramcontent.com/pod-product-compliance
Lightning Source LLC
Chambersburg PA
CBHW040855010826
48978CB00013BA/1029